Sunny

Richelle.

Nick

ELMO

LIZ

EMILY RODDA'S
RAVEN HILL MYSTERIES

CASE #5: DIRTY TRICKS

**Be on the lookout for all of
Emily Rodda's Raven Hill Mysteries**

EMILY RODDA'S
RAVEN HILL MYSTERIES

CASE #5: DIRTY TRICKS

Emily Rodda and Kate Rowe

SCHOLASTIC INC.

New York Toronto London Auckland Sydney
Mexico City New Delhi Hong Kong Buenos Aires

No part of this publication may be reproduced, stored in a retrieval system, or transmitted in any form or by any means, electronic, mechanical, photocopying, recording, or otherwise, without written permission of the publisher. For information regarding permission, write to Permissions Department, Scholastic Australia, P.O. Box 579, Lindfield, New South Wales, Australia 2070.

ISBN 0-439-79571-0

Series concept copyright © 1994 by Emily Rodda
Text copyright © 1997 by Scholastic Australia Pty. Limited

All rights reserved. Published by Scholastic Inc., 557 Broadway, New York, NY 10012, by arrangement with Scholastic Press, an imprint of Scholastic Australia.

SCHOLASTIC, APPLE PAPERBACKS, and associated logos are trademarks and/or registered trademarks of Scholastic Inc.

12 11 10 9 8 7 6   11/0

Printed in the U.S.A.
First American edition, July 2006

EMILY RODDA'S
RAVEN HILL MYSTERIES

CASE #5: DIRTY TRICKS

Contents

1

The mystery begins

To me, the Raven Hill Library used to be two things — very old and incredibly boring. All my life, people had been saying it was haunted, and that didn't surprise me a bit. I was certain it was *full* of ghosts — cranky librarians and their victims who had died of boredom.

But recently, everything I thought about Raven Hill Library was turned upside down. And I was taken completely by surprise. I could never have imagined a practical joker prowling around those dusty old shelves. And even when everyone in Raven Hill was talking about the tricks, I never could have guessed what was going to happen next.

Trouble, basically. That's what was going to happen. And as usual, I was in it up to my neck — thanks to Help-for-Hire Inc.

Help-for-Hire Inc. is the part-time job agency that my friend Liz Free set up to earn us some spending money. By "us" I mean Liz and me — I'm Richelle Brinkley — plus four other friends — Sunny Chan, Nick Kontellis, Tom Moysten, and Elmo Zimmer.

Ever since Help-for-Hire Inc. started, I've had no peace. That's because, more often than not, it's not just cash, but catastrophe that comes our way. Somehow, just by doing the most ordinary jobs, like handing out leaflets or walking a dog, we manage to get involved in the weirdest mysteries.

It's all the others' fault. They should be more like me and not get so involved in things. Liz is so sympathetic — it gets her talking to the strangest people and wanting to help them. Nick, Tom, and Elmo are all incredibly curious, even though they're so different in other ways. Sunny's the only one who doesn't usually start trouble. She's just good at getting us out of it.

I know what Liz would say if she read this. And I guess she'd be right. What happened at the library would have happened whether or not we were working there. But all the same, we were in it — right from the start.

Not everyone I know finds libraries as boring as I did to begin with. But everyone I know would agree with one basic thing.

A library is not supposed to be a dangerous place.

❂

It all started at Raven Hill High — in class, one cold, rainy Monday morning. Our new English teacher, Mr. Raven, was giving us an assignment. As if a rainy Monday morning wasn't bad enough.

Mr. Raven was weird. He wore a dark suit and black-framed rectangular glasses. He was very thin and pale, and he had straight, shoulder-length black hair and big, pale green eyes.

He didn't look like your average teacher, in other words. He didn't seem to have that awful, bright enthusiasm that most new teachers have, either. His voice was soft and low and never changed tone at all. It never went up, and it never went down.

In fact, there was something quite spooky about him. A few of the guys at the back of the class had tried to give him a hard time early in the lesson. But he'd just kind of looked at them with those pale green eyes and they shut up.

He handed out photocopied sheets to everyone. I looked at my copy. It was titled "Alphabetical Mysteries." Underneath was a list of words in alphabetical order: *Alphabet, Bees, Chameleon, Doughnut,* and so on, all the way down to *Zodiac.*

Mr. Raven told us that since there were twenty-six of us in the class, and twenty-six letters in the alphabet, there was one topic on the list for each of us.

"A most fortunate coincidence," he said softly, pushing his hair behind his ears with long, bony fingers. "I am very fond of the alphabet." His thin lips curved in what I guess was a smile. It was a weird, curvy smile that didn't show his teeth.

I looked at Liz and Nick, who were sitting on my left. We've been stuck with some weird teachers before, but it looked like Mr. Raven was going to be the worst yet. Nick rolled his eyes back at me, and Liz covered a smile with her hand.

"You are each to choose one of these topics and research it at Raven Hill Library," Mr. Raven went on. "It's very important to develop good library skills. It is also good to support your local library by using it regularly."

"And by paying library fines," groaned Tom on my right, as he sketched cartoons of Mr. Raven all over his list of topics. I pretended I hadn't heard him. For days we'd been hearing about Tom's lost library book and getting updates of everywhere he'd looked for it. I never listened when he got started. If only he'd be a bit more organized, he wouldn't get himself into these messes.

"As I told you all when I introduced myself," continued Mr. Raven, perching carefully on the edge of his desk, "until a few weeks ago I worked part time at Raven Hill Library. So I know that they have books on all these topics."

I gazed at the clock helplessly and listened to the rain beating down outside. I hate assignments. And these topics were really weird. *E* for Elephant. *F* for Fingerprint. *G* for Gypsy. Apart from the fact that they were all in a list together, they seemed to have nothing else in common.

Fortunately, I wasn't the only one who was confused.

"These topics are all very different from one another, Mr. Raven," said Sunny's flat, practical voice from the row in front of me. "I don't really understand what we have to do."

Mr. Raven gave that strange little smile again and sat up straighter on the edge of his desk.

"The assignment title is the clue," he said. "'Alphabetical Mysteries.' You'll find that every one of the topics on this list involves some kind of mystery."

A flash of lightning lit up the room and I jumped. He paused until the thunder crashed a second or two later, and a shiver ran up and down my spine. He didn't have to be so dark and spooky in the middle of a storm! Not when there were people as sensitive as me in the class. I get spooked really easily.

"Mystery?" said Elmo, who was sitting next to Sunny. I could see him leaning forward on his desk. I could just imagine his eyes sparkling. Trust Elmo to be interested.

Mr. Raven nodded. "There is something about each of these topics that is not widely known, or not fully understood, or is just surprising or unusual," he said.

"How come *P* is for Phobia instead of Phantom, then?" some idiot called out from the back. Bradley Henshaw, probably.

Everyone snickered. Thanks to our local paper, the *Pen*, everyone knew about the so-called Phantom of the Library, and the tricks he had been playing for the last month. Everyone thought they were so funny. Everyone but me, that is.

Mr. Raven ignored the interruption. "I have my own ideas," he went on. "But it's up to each of you to choose your topic and then discover and describe the mystery that *you* see within it."

It sounded pretty boring to me. I looked at the list again. I couldn't see anything mysterious about most of these topics. Elephants? Elephants are elephants. Doughnut? What's mysterious about a doughnut? It's fattening. It's round. That's all.

"When's it due?" asked Nick, getting down to basics.

"Next Monday," answered Mr. Raven briefly.

Just a week! There was a bit of complaining about that, but he raised his hand for silence. "The research won't take long," he said calmly. "Then you only have to write as much as you need to explain the mystery. And give a list of the books you've used to discover it."

I wriggled uncomfortably on my chair.

"I suggest you waste no time in choosing your topic," said Mr. Raven as the bell rang. I sprang to my feet in relief. I couldn't wait to get out of there.

To my surprise, most of the other kids crowded around Mr. Raven's desk, all of them hoping for their first choices. Some of them seemed really excited.

"X! X! I want X!" I heard Tom yell. I checked my sheet. X-ray.

"X-ray. Of course. It couldn't be anything else. Except Xylophone, I suppose," I said gloomily.

"What about Xylem? Or Xenophobia?" asked Elmo.

I mumbled "mmm" to make it seem like I knew what those words meant and left without putting my name down for anything. The thunder rumbled loudly, like a warning that trouble lay ahead.

I should have listened to it.

2

Enter the Phantom

"I thought teachers were supposed to teach *us* stuff, not get us to teach ourselves," I grumbled that afternoon. We were all sitting in the Black Cat Cafe. Outside, it was freezing, and the rain was pouring down in buckets. I was looking again at Mr. Raven's list, now crumpled from being stuffed angrily into my bag.

"But that's the point," argued Liz. "For once we get to really use our brains and think for ourselves. It's great."

"Yeah," said Elmo. "This is going to be the most interesting assignment I've had all year!"

I stared at him. I couldn't believe it. He was actually serious!

"This is so unfair," I complained. "I was looking forward to a relaxed weekend. Now I'll be stuck doing this."

"It's Monday afternoon, and you're already looking forward to the weekend?" Sunny giggled.

Well, so what if I was? What was so strange about that?

"Richelle, if you start tomorrow, you could get the whole thing finished and ready before the weekend even starts," said Liz. I suppose she was trying to comfort me. But she *knows* I can never make myself do homework till the last minute.

"*P* for Phobia is interesting. But I really wanted X," grumbled Tom, who had apparently missed out. "I've got X-rays at home from when I broke my arm. And talk about mystery . . ."

The missing book again. I tuned out and started looking at my fingernails. The only mystery I was interested in was how my nail polish had gotten chipped. I couldn't remember it happening. I could only imagine that I'd done it fidgeting in class while Mr. Raven was talking. It was all his fault.

By the time I started listening again, Sunny was talking. "When my sister was studying medicine she was out almost every night looking things up," she said, "at the university library."

"Don't say that around Raven," groaned Tom. "The university library's huge. He'll make us go there, and I'll get lost and never be seen again!"

Elmo laughed. "Come on, Tom," he said, "it's not that hard to get around a library. The way you talk you'd think the Dewey System had never been invented!"

"Ah yes, the Dewey Decimal System," breathed Tom in an awed voice. "Oh yes, Elmo, chosen one, he who understands the mysteries of Dewey! All hail!" He made a deep bow to Elmo.

Elmo frowned. He doesn't like being teased about being so brainy, though he brings it on himself. Especially when he uses words like *xylem* that no one else has ever heard of.

"I don't understand that stupid system, either," I muttered into my cup.

"Oh, Richelle, of course you do," said Liz, spooning a half-melted marshmallow from her hot chocolate into her mouth. "Don't you remember playing those Find the Section games in the library with Miss Spicer? When we were in third grade?"

"Sort of," I said. "I remember that Miss Spicer was as horrible and crabby then as she is now, and I got into trouble because I didn't want to play." I thought about it some more. "And I remember that you won the game and got a bookmark."

"Yes, I did," Liz said smugly.

"And boasted about it for a week," I added.

Tom snickered, and Liz put her nose in the air.

"Miss Spicer isn't horrible *or* cranky, Richelle," she snapped. "You're just still annoyed about that time in fourth grade when she told you off for bringing your books back late and you cried."

Tom snorted with laughter, Nick smirked, and Sunny giggled. Sometimes Liz has the biggest mouth in the world.

"It's got nothing to do with that," I said, flicking my hair over my shoulder in what I hoped was a dignified manner. "I just don't like her. She acts all superior, as if she thinks she's queen of the books or something. And she doesn't like me."

"Poor little Richelle," snickered Tom, slurping his hot chocolate.

That made me mad.

"You can't laugh, Tom. She'll like you even less than she likes me, now that you've lost that book," I snapped.

That took the grin off his face.

"It's disappeared into thin air," he moaned. "It's probably sprouted legs and run back to the library to hide."

"Yeah, right," said Nick sarcastically, but Liz smiled.

"That's not so unlikely, considering what's been happening lately," she said. "The Phantom might have put a spell on it."

Tom thudded his drink down on the table so hard that a few

drops flew out and splashed me. "That's it!" he exclaimed. "I could blame it all on the Phantom!"

"Miss Spicer won't swallow it," said Sunny. "The Phantom doesn't play tricks outside the library, Tom. Only in it."

So then, of course, they all started talking about the Phantom and the latest tricks they'd heard about.

I sighed. I hadn't wanted to talk about Mr. Raven's stupid assignment, but I wanted to talk about the Phantom even less. I hadn't said anything to the others, but the whole idea of the Phantom gave me the creeps. I couldn't understand why everyone else thought it was all so much fun. Every week now, the *Pen* had some silly headline like "Library Phantom Strikes Again!" And just about every day someone at school was talking about the latest Phantom joke.

Someone in our class had been at the library the first time it happened. They'd gone to the library as soon as it opened in the morning to borrow a book before school started. Sitting on a desk near the art section was a toy kitten. It had been painted every color of the rainbow and actually held a wet paintbrush in its paw.

The weirdest thing was that there was a book called *How to Paint Cats* sitting in front of the toy. It was as if, in the middle of the night, the painted cat had followed the instructions inside the book — or had actually jumped out of the book. No one had seen anyone set the thing up. It was a complete mystery.

A few days later, when Liz's little brother Pete went on a library excursion, they found a book called *The Wonderful World of Frogs* lying open on the floor in the nature section. Pete said there were masses of chocolate frogs sitting on the book and all around on the carpet, as if they had come to life and jumped right out of the book.

Once the amazement had passed, those chocolate frogs didn't have a chance, of course. Pete's class gobbled them fast.

After that, things kept happening all the time. Some innocent person would pull a book on astronomy from a shelf, for example, and little silver stars would fall out all over the floor. Or someone would find *The World's Funniest Jokes* open on a table with one of those stupid joke shop laughing machines in a bag lying on top and laughing its head off.

Then the *Pen* got a hold of the story and made a great big deal about it. They called the practical joker "the Phantom of the Library," and pretty soon everyone was talking about him. I say "him" because most people did, but we all knew that the Phantom could just as easily have been "her." The Phantom's identity was still a complete mystery.

The one thing that was very clear was that the Phantom's jokes all had something to do with books. The Phantom was obsessed with them.

People kept writing to the *Pen* about tricks they'd seen or discovered, giving their theories about who the Phantom was. Elmo's father runs the *Pen*, and Help-for-Hire Inc. delivers it around Raven Hill every week. So we couldn't help hearing about the Phantom all the time, whether we wanted to or not.

At school, it became quite a big deal to be able to tell Elmo that someone you knew had found one of the jokes or, even better, that you had. A lot of kids went to the library for the first time in years, especially to see if they could discover one of the Phantom's little tricks. And a lot of them did. Elmo wrote down all the jokes. Then they were published in the *Pen*.

The *Pen* had interviewed Miss Spicer. She'd admitted that she had no idea who the Phantom was. But it was obvious that she quite liked his jokes. And she used the interview to put in a little ad for reading.

"I've been thinking about it," she said, "and it seems to me that there is a lot more to books than people realize. They have a special power. Reading a book can take you to any time and to any place in the world — or beyond! If that's not power, what is?"

I didn't know about that. Apart from having a special power to bore me, I didn't think that books were anything special. That meant I was probably the only person in Raven Hill who wasn't interested in the Phantom's jokes. Even cool Nick had been sucked in.

"My favorite was *Buying and Selling for Profit* filled with play money," he was saying now.

"My favorite was the *Alice in Wonderland* one, with the teapot and the dirty cups and saucers all around the Borrowing Desk like the Mad Hatter's tea party," Liz said.

Elmo nodded. "I got a photo of that one for the *Pen*. I was lucky, because Mr. Kelly, that assistant librarian guy, came home from vacation the next day and nagged Miss Spicer into cleaning it up. She wanted to leave it on display. I think it's been the best one so far, too."

"No way," said Tom. "The best one was the *Encyclopedia of*

Diseases, with the thermometer tucked inside the cover, and red spots stuck all over it like measles."

And so it went on for ages.

"I wish I could find one of the jokes," sighed Tom finally.

"Well, we'll be spending a lot of time in the library in the next few days," Elmo reminded him. "I'll bet one of us finds something while we're there."

Unfortunately, he was right. And even more unfortunately, that someone turned out to be me.

3

The library

The others basically forced me to go and choose a topic the next day at lunchtime.

"Otherwise, you'll get stuck with a topic you hate, Richelle," warned Sunny.

"I hate them all," I grumbled.

"This way you can come to the library with us after school today and make a good start, nice and early," urged Liz.

The English faculty room was on the third floor of the main building. It was so boring climbing all those stairs.

As I knocked on the faculty room door, I thought about the topic I'd decided on. *T* for Tutankhamen. Tutankhamen was a king of Egypt. A Pharaoh. At least I knew what his mystery was. I'd seen a really spooky TV show about a curse that struck all the people who opened Tutankhamen's tomb.

I was too late.

"Sorry, Richelle," said Mr. Raven, pale green eyes glancing down his list. "Sunny Chan has already chosen that one."

"Oh," I said, surprised. Sunny hadn't said anything about that in the Black Cat Cafe. Or maybe she had, while I was looking at my nail polish. I should have paid more attention. I glanced quickly at the sheet again.

"Um . . . well, then I'll choose *B*. For Bees," I said quickly. At least it would be easy to find information on bees.

"Sorry, Richelle, but that's taken, too," he said. "They're all taken except *D* for Doughnut."

"Doughnut," I repeated, disgusted.

"I thought the list was a bit too serious, so I added a few funny topics. That's a funny topic, don't you think, Richelle?" said Mr. Raven, sweeping imaginary crumbs off his suit with pale, bony fingers.

I didn't. This guy was *so* weird.

"Well, what's so mysterious about doughnuts?" I blurted out.

"Think about it," he said. "I'm sure if you think about it and read about it, you'll work it out. You'll work the *whole* thing out." And this time his smile showed two rows of pointy yellow teeth.

I was out of there pretty quickly. I trudged away, back down the hallway, feeling worse than I had before.

The bell rang as I got to the bottom of the stairs. On the way to class, Liz asked me what I'd chosen for my topic, but I said that I didn't want to talk about it. I could just imagine how they'd all make fun of me if I told them what I'd been stuck with. Doughnuts. It was just ridiculous.

✿

When the bell rang for the end of school, I walked to the library in the rain with Liz, Tom, and Sunny.

Liz and Tom were walking under Liz's red umbrella with

holes in it, in front of Sunny and me. Luckily, Liz was too busy arguing with Tom about who should hold the umbrella to notice how depressed I was.

"Tom, just give it to me! When you hold it, you wave it around and the water drips onto my neck. Stop it! Stop it!" she shrieked. She grabbed the umbrella from Tom. Then he started complaining.

"Liz, you're too short. My head keeps bumping against the top," he whined.

"Well, bend your knees," she said unsympathetically.

"Why don't you just grow a bit?"

He tried to grab the umbrella again, and Liz started slapping his hands, trying to loosen his grip. Wet weather really brings out the worst in people. It was quite embarrassing. Sunny and I walked calmly under my umbrella without a single problem.

"What did you choose, anyway, Richelle?" she asked me.

"Um . . . it's sort of . . . a surprise," I said weakly.

She just nodded. Sometimes Sunny irritates me because she's so calm about everything. But on this occasion I was grateful.

I kicked my feet along the ground and stared crossly at the back of Tom's head, thinking that *D* for Doughnut sounded much more like his kind of assignment. He's obsessed with junk food and eats tons of it.

"You chose Tutankhamen, didn't you?" I asked Sunny.

She nodded. "At least I know what that mystery is. And there weren't any topics about sports."

Sunny loves sports. Any kind of sports. She probably really enjoyed the walk to the library, which wasn't very long, but was up a very steep hill. I didn't. I was feeling as though I was going to burst by the time we finally arrived.

I peeked out from under the umbrella. The entrance to Raven Hill Library towered above me, and lightning flashed against its windows.

The library is one of the oldest buildings in Raven Hill. So although it was painted only a few years ago, it still seems dark — and creepy — with a damp, booky sort of smell. The libraries in some of the places near us, like Linvale, are new, clean, and modern. I knew I'd feel much better about visiting them.

I reluctantly followed the others inside, through the old wooden doors with their weird carvings, through the foyer, and into the flickering fluorescent light of the main reading room. It was really quiet. As usual. That's another thing I don't like about libraries.

Blue carpet stretched ahead of us, turning right to the borrowing desk and the stairs, running straight ahead to the computer terminals and then farther on to the shelves of books, and past the desks and chairs. I knew that up the stairs was another floor they called "the attic," where the oldest and rarest books were kept in glass cases.

Nick had already arrived and was sitting at one of the computers. He waved at us self-consciously as we came in, and we went over to him. Looking around the library, I could see that quite a few other people from Mr. Raven's English class were there, too.

No one seemed to mind being in the library. No one was a bit worried about the Phantom.

But I was. I kept thinking about the old stories of the library being haunted. And about how no one would own up to setting up the Phantom's jokes, and no one could catch anyone else doing it.

What if there wasn't a Phantom at all?

What if it was the books? What if somehow they were coming to life?

I couldn't tell the others. I could just imagine what Nick would say. "Books coming to life? Yeah, right, Richelle!"

Tom and Sunny would laugh. And Liz would look worried, as if she thought I was going completely nuts.

But even if I couldn't say anything, I couldn't stop thinking about it. It gave me a creepy feeling thinking about the books running around in the middle of the night.

Little did I know that by the end of all this I'd have a lot more than a creepy feeling to be worried about.

A lot more.

4

Teddy bears' adventure

Liz sat down at one of the other computer terminals and started looking up books on her topic. She was doing *E* for Elephant. I wasn't surprised. She's very interested in animals and nature and saving the world.

I peeped over her shoulder and watched her select "Search by Subject" and then type in "elephant." I figured out that since I didn't know the name of any books about doughnuts I'd have to do a "Search by Subject," too. Liz pressed the ENTER key, and three books came up on the screen, each with its own reference number. She squeaked with excitement when she saw the last one, *The Elephants' Graveyard.*

"I can't believe there's actually a book all about the elephants' graveyard," she exclaimed, scribbling down all three numbers. "It's such a mystery! Does it really exist? How do they know where to go to die? Oh, this is going to be so interesting!"

"Mmm," I said. An elephant graveyard. Sounded fascinating.

I could tell she was going to offer to help me find my books, but luckily Elmo walked into the library at just that moment. He had his camera with him.

"Oh, look, there's Elmo," said Liz. "I thought he was at the *Pen* this afternoon. Why's he brought his camera?" She ran off to find out. I was relieved. I was embarrassed enough to be typing "doughnut" into the computer, without Liz being there to see it.

I couldn't make the chair move at all, so I had to slide into it to sit down. After making the computer beep angrily a few times, I worked out how to do my search. The word "doughnut" didn't bring up any entries at all. I didn't know what to do next. I tried typing in "icing" and "chocolate sprinkles," but they didn't work, either. So I gave up.

It wasn't my fault. Obviously the library just didn't have anything on doughnuts, whatever Mr. Raven said. At least I had a good excuse not to start the stupid project.

"Richelle!" Liz was hissing at me from the other side of the room. I looked up. She was beckoning excitedly. Behind her, Tom, Nick, and Elmo were heading up the stairs to the attic. What was going on? I slid out of the chair and went to join her.

"Elmo says there's a really good Phantom joke in the attic," Liz whispered as I reached her. "Come up and see."

I didn't want to go, but she insisted, and, after all, there was nothing else to do. I followed her reluctantly up the stairs.

I hadn't been in the Raven Hill Library attic since I was about six. It's the only part of the upstairs that's open to the public — a tiny room, strangely shaped, with a low ceiling. Tom had to bend his head to get through the door. Along every wall are glass cases, filled with old, serious-looking books. When I was young, it scared me.

But now the room was a bit happier. A big fluffy brown

teddy bear sat on top of one of the glass cases, holding onto a rope. Halfway up the rope was another teddy bear, who seemed to be in the middle of climbing up. Both bears wore helmets made from empty ice-cream containers. And lying open on top of the case was an old children's storybook: *Teddy Bears' Adventure*.

"Cute," said Nick dryly, arms folded.

Elmo took a photograph of the bears. Then, when some little kids came up the stairs, he took a photo of them looking at the bears. "For the *Pen*," he explained as we made our way carefully back down the steep stairs. "Miss Spicer called Dad about it at lunchtime. We can use this in Thursday's edition."

Miss Spicer came scuttling toward us from the front desk. I was surprised to see how small she was. She'd looked much bigger when I was a little kid. Now I was quite a bit taller than she was. And I must say, she didn't look as fierce as I'd remembered, either.

Her gray hair was pinned back in a bun, but wisps of it had come undone and were waving madly around her head and face. Nick and I tried to edge away, but Elmo and Liz were in the way and they weren't budging. I noticed Tom had already escaped.

"You've been to see the bears?" she asked us, smiling. Her little black eyes flicked rapidly across each of our faces. She made no sign that she recognized me. I suppose I've changed a lot since grade school.

"Yes, Miss Spicer," said Elmo politely. "I took a photograph for the *Pen*. The bears were in the attic when you opened up this morning, weren't they?"

"Well, I'm not sure, Elmo dear," she fluttered. "They weren't found till eleven-thirty or so, when someone went upstairs. No one had been up to the attic until then. So we don't exactly know how or when the bears got there."

Just then, a tall, skinny man came over. He had a bushy mustache and long, tousled hair. He wore a badge that read ASSISTANT LIBRARIAN that shone proudly on his shirt pocket. He had a bald patch that seemed to shine quite proudly, too.

"Mary, I've been trying to catch you," he said, looking down at her from his great height. I noticed that his mustache wiggled when he talked, which looked rather funny. "I really think it's time we took those bears in the attic down. It's dangerous, all those kids running around up there. Those are valuable books, and . . ."

Miss Spicer's kind, blank expression vanished, and I saw her little black eyes flash and her fists clench. *Now* she looked fierce.

"I don't agree, Pierce," she said sharply. "The children like the bears. And why shouldn't they look at the rare books at the same time? That's what the books are there for. Now, I must have a word with Frankie." And she scuttled off toward her desk.

The man heaved a big sigh.

"All it takes is for someone to trip and fall over up there, and the library will take the blame," he muttered. He ran a hand over his bald spot. At least he was honest about having one. I hate it when men comb their only remaining hairs across their bald heads.

"I'm sure there's no need to worry, Mr. Kelly," said Elmo. "No one's likely to trip over a teddy bear."

The assistant librarian laughed, but the laugh had a hollow sound to it. "You can't be too careful, ah, Alvin," he said.

"Elmo," said Elmo, correcting him.

"Yes. Right," said Mr. Kelly, embarrassed, and he strode away.

"How long's he been here?" I hissed in Elmo's ear as we walked quietly back toward the shelves.

"About a year — maybe eighteen months," he said. "Why?"

"He and Miss Spicer don't seem to like each other much," I said.

"They don't!" Liz put in, in a low voice. "It's a shame. They've both got their good points. If they'd only cooperate —"

Elmo shook his curly head. "They'll never cooperate," he said definitely. "This Phantom thing has really pointed out their differences. Mr. Kelly likes everything really neat and well organized, so he hates it. He thinks it makes the staff look silly. Miss Spicer doesn't care how silly she looks. She thinks the Phantom's jokes are funny, and she likes the way they're attracting people to the library."

"I'll bet she wishes she knew who the Phantom was, all the same," I said.

"Maybe she's the Phantom herself," hissed Tom, appearing suddenly from behind a bookshelf and nearly giving me a heart attack.

"What are you doing skulking around like that?" I asked crossly.

He shrugged. "I don't want old Spicer to see me. She'll ask

23

me about that book that's so late. I've got to keep out of her way. Until I finish this assignment, anyway."

He showed us the armful of books that he had already collected. "I'm going to be the teacher's pet for sure with this stack," he joked.

"I think that bonus points will go to whomever was crazy enough to choose A for Alphabet," I said.

Elmo cleared his throat. Oh, no.

"Sorry, I didn't know you'd chosen it," I said miserably. Was nothing going to go right today?

But he wasn't offended. "It's okay, Richelle. I know you wouldn't find it interesting, but I like words and writing and all that sort of thing, you know."

I knew. Elmo is definitely going to end up being a writer or a journalist or something. It's in his blood, and he's really smart. His clothes are never neat, his hair is always messy, and sometimes he gets tongue-tied when he talks. But I guess on paper that sort of thing doesn't matter.

"Don't judge a book by its cover, Richelle," Liz said to me once. "To you it's important to look nice. But it's what's inside a person that counts."

I thought about that as we walked toward a group of free desks. "I suppose even Mr. Raven isn't as weird as he looks," I said aloud. I don't know quite why I was thinking about Mr. Raven at just this minute, but I was.

"I don't know about that," grinned Tom. "If you ask me he's stark Raven mad."

He paused, while everyone laughed at the weak joke. He'd

probably thought of it ages ago and been waiting for a chance to make it, I thought.

"Poor Mr. Raven," exclaimed Liz. "He's not so weird."

"How about him taking attendance backward this morning?" asked Nick.

Tom nodded and imitated Mr. Raven's slow, monotonous voice: "I just want to give Z a turn at being first, for once," he said, wrinkling his forehead and tucking imaginary hair behind his ears.

"He *is* weird," I said.

"After this morning, I think he's great," said Elmo. "So would you, if your name was Zimmer. I'm always last in everything. This morning, thanks to Raven Mad, I was first."

I tried to pull a chair out from the table — and couldn't.

"What is this?" I complained, yanking at it.

"All the chairs are connected to the tables, Richelle," said Elmo. "Even the front desk. It was Mr. Kelly's idea. To keep people from leaving chairs all over the place."

"Well, it's a stupid idea," I snapped.

I left them and started just wandering around the shelves. Then I saw with a shock that Mr. Raven was at the front desk with Miss Spicer and Mr. Kelly. He was gripping a large painting in his pale, thin fingers.

What was he doing here?

5

Unkindness

"But why, Mary?" Mr. Raven was asking. "I painted it especially for the library. To fill that blank wall above the desk here." He looked pleadingly at her.

"It's very kind of you, Mark, but I really have to say no," said Miss Spicer bluntly. "It's much too gloomy. It'll scare the visitors."

Mr. Raven looked crushed. It was a really embarrassing moment. I couldn't see why Miss Spicer just didn't take the painting. It was free. And from what I could see it was just a painting of a black bird, a raven. What was so wrong with that?

"It's a dignified painting, Mary," I heard Mr. Kelly say. "Dignified and . . . serious. It could be just what we need."

"Yes," urged Mr. Raven, recovering a bit. "It might help make a good impression on the supervisor, Mary. Help you keep your job —"

"*What?*" Miss Spicer's voice was dangerously calm.

I stood frozen, unsure of whether to walk away or stand still.

"Oh," said Mr. Raven, looking uncertainly at Mr. Kelly. "Pierce said . . . I thought you . . ."

"I didn't want to worry you, Mary," said Mr. Pierce, teeth clenched in a grim smile. "But I don't think the supervisor was very happy after the visit on Friday."

"Why didn't you say something to me?" Miss Spicer was icy now.

Mr. Kelly ran his hand over his shiny bald patch. "Well, frankly, Mary, it's because you just don't listen to me. It's like I said. People want a library to be orderly, neat, and tidy. In control. This stupid Phantom business is making us all a laughingstock. And you encourage it."

"If I do, it's because I can see that it's doing the library good!" hissed Miss Spicer.

Mr. Kelly drew himself up to his full height. "Well," he said, "I don't think the supervisor agrees. In my opinion, if you don't get this place into shape . . ."

I didn't want to hear anymore. I turned around to leave. But as soon as I moved, they glanced in my direction. Then I had no choice but to walk right up to the desk and smile, pretending I hadn't heard a thing.

Mr. Raven recognized me, and I thought I saw a spark of panic in his eyes. To cover my own embarrassment, I looked at the painting. I was all ready to praise it, but then I saw it properly. The bird's beak was wide open. Its yellow eyes stared. It looked as if it was in pain. Other ravens lay twisted in the background. It was very depressing.

"Oh!" I heard myself exclaim. Then I didn't know what to say.

"It's a fine piece of work," said Mr. Kelly.

"It's well painted but very unpleasant," snapped Miss Spicer.

"Painting seems to bring the worst out in you, Mark. You should stick to poetry."

Mr. Kelly and Mr. Raven stared at her in silence, and, suddenly, she seemed to give up. She flapped her hands crossly. "Oh, all right!" she snapped. "It can go in the attic, if you insist. Hardly anyone goes up there, anyway."

Mr. Raven just looked at her for another moment, then turned and left without saying another word.

"Mary, that wasn't very nice," said Mr. Kelly in frustration.

"*Nice?*" she hissed. "I'm past being nice, Pierce. What did you mean by —"

At this point she seemed to remember I was there. She gave me a confused sort of smile.

"Hang up the painting, Pierce," she said to Mr. Kelly in a low voice. "You'll have to do it. I can't, now that the ladder is broken, and neither can Frankie. And you're the one who wanted the thing, anyway."

She turned to me. "Would you mind helping Mr. Kelly, dear?"

But Mr. Kelly was already striding away toward the stairs with the painting under one arm. I hurried after him.

"She has no *idea* what's good for this library," he was muttering to himself when I caught up with him. His mustache was quivering in anger.

I followed helplessly as he pounded up the stairs. Then there was a dull thump, and he gave a furious yell. He'd bumped his head on the low attic door. The little kids beside the bears giggled.

"Get out of here," he snarled at them, still furious from the

28

bump on his head. They bolted for the stairs, terrified. Mr. Kelly touched the top of his head, which now had a bright red spot in the middle of the bald patch.

"I think you're going to get a bruise," I said helpfully. He didn't answer, which I thought was quite rude. He hung the painting on a hook that was sticking out high on one of the walls, then disappeared down the stairs again.

He'd left the painting hanging crookedly. I stood on my toes and did my best to straighten it. I tried not to look too hard at the tormented bird, but its yellow eyes seemed to follow every move I made.

The painting was really quite horrible. And I noticed for the first time that the title, engraved on the frame, was "Unkindness."

I wondered if Mr. Raven thought of himself as that bird. The thought sent a chill up my back. Feeling awful, I left the attic and went down the stairs again. I decided to go to the ladies' room and do my hair. Doing my hair always helps me to calm down.

But not this time. Remember I said earlier that I was the first of my friends to find a practical joke in the library? Well, I didn't mean the teddy bears' adventure. I was talking about the bucket of water that fell on my head as I walked through the door of the ladies' room.

✿

I must have yelled pretty loudly, because Liz and Sunny came running in almost right away. I had slipped in the water and was sitting on the floor with the bucket lying next to me. My forehead hurt. I think the bucket's handle had whacked me as it fell.

"Richelle! What happened?" shrieked Liz.

Sunny helped me to my feet and tried to brush some of the water off my clothes. I was so shocked that I could barely speak. My elbow really hurt, right on the funny bone. I could sort of remember landing on it.

"It fell. On my head," I managed to say stupidly.

"That's so weird," said Liz. "I was in here ten minutes ago, and there was nothing here then."

"What's going on in there?" yelled Mr. Kelly's voice from outside.

"I think you'd better come and sit down, Richelle," said Sunny calmly. "You're very pale. Your forehead's bleeding a bit. Come on."

They helped me out of the bathroom, and Sunny made me sit down on a chair with my head between my knees. It made me feel a bit less dizzy.

"What are you kids doing?" thundered Mr. Raven's voice. "A library is a place of silence, not —"

"Quiet, Pierce!" said Miss Spicer's voice. I looked up and saw her among a big crowd. The faces blurred together as I stared dizzily around at everyone.

"What happened, dear?" Miss Spicer asked me.

"A bucket of water fell on my head when I went into the ladies' room," I whispered.

"There's water everywhere," said Sunny. "And I saw something on the bench. . . ."

She went back into the bathroom, and Miss Spicer leaned over toward Elmo.

"Run and get Frankie, Elmo dear," she said. "He'll be in the storeroom. Ask him to bring the first aid kit."

Elmo nodded and sped off to the storeroom behind the stairs. Liz was patting my hand. Sunny came out of the ladies' room carrying a large, open book, which she showed to the librarian. Miss Spicer put her glasses on with hands that shook a bit. She was obviously shocked.

"*Bible Stories for Children*," read Liz, craning her neck to look at the cover of the book.

"Opened at the story of Noah's ark," said Miss Spicer, slowly. Suddenly, everyone was exchanging glances.

"I don't understand. What's Noah's ark got to do with me getting a bucket of water tipped all over me?" I asked, confused.

"Well, you know the story, don't you? There was a flood. It rained for forty days and forty nights," said Nick. "Lots of water. Get it?"

"Looks like the Phantom has struck again!" said Tom in that deep spooky voice he likes to do.

"It was a pretty mean, stupid sort of trick if you ask me," I said weakly.

And that was only the beginning.

31

6

Clowning around

"All right, nothing more to see," said Mr. Kelly to the gathered crowd. "Please move along now." He was doing his best to be stern and dignified, but the large red bump right in the center of his bald head spoiled his image. Some people drifted away a bit, but most stayed right where they were, watching.

"This is awful!" fretted Miss Spicer. "I'm so sorry, Richelle." So she did remember me.

"Is there anything you want?" asked Mr. Kelly. "Anything at all?"

He was probably being nice to me because he was worried that I was going to sue the library. But all I wanted was to go home.

"Ambulance coming through!" A little man in overalls, making a noise like a siren and carrying a small white case with a red cross on it, pushed through the crowd. He screeched like brakes, kneeled down beside me, and opened the case. I don't think I've ever been so embarrassed in my life.

I knew this must be Frankie. His badge said FRANKIE BELA, CARETAKER. Elmo took some photographs as the man opened the little case and pulled out some antiseptic cream.

"You vulture," grinned Nick to Elmo. "What a scoop for the *Pen!*"

"Put that camera away at once!" ordered Mr. Kelly. "We don't want to encourage this madman with any more publicity!" Elmo looked annoyed, but did what he said.

"It's not so bad," said Frankie, looking at the cut on my forehead. "You'll be all right, dear. Won't leave a scar or nothing. I had far worse than this back in the circus."

"Frankie was a clown, you know, Richelle," said Liz, watching him dab antiseptic cream onto the cut.

Frankie winked at me and grinned widely. His eyes were very bright blue against his tanned, leathery skin. "Never have guessed, would ya?" he said.

For a second I forgot to be embarrassed and smiled back at him. But when he pulled a bandage out of the first aid kit, I shrank back against the chair.

"Oh, no," I said, trying to shake my head and finding that it hurt. "No way am I having a bandage on my forehead!"

"Richelle, for goodness' sake!" said Liz fiercely. "Now is not the time to be worried about your looks!"

"Wear it like a badge of honor, like we did back in the circus," suggested Frankie. He firmly fastened the bandage right across the middle of my forehead. I heard snickers and looked up to see that my so-called friends were trying not to laugh.

"Think positive, Richelle," said Liz brightly. "You don't look nearly as silly as Tom did when he had that big Band-Aid right across his nose."

"Hey!" said Tom, annoyed. Nick laughed even harder.

"Did I say anything, Liz, *anything* at all when you had that huge pimple on the end of *your* nose last week?" Tom demanded passionately.

Now Liz looked offended, and I secretly smiled. She'd rejected my tactful offer of pimple concealer quite rudely at the time.

Nick was laughing so much that he had tears coming out of his eyes. Nick hardly ever gets pimples.

"Shut up, Nick," said Tom and Liz at the same time, arms folded with their backs to each other.

Frankie put another bandage on my elbow, which was a bit scraped. He straightened up. He was really short — no taller than little Miss Spicer, though stockier than her, of course. He jerked his head in the direction of my friends.

"Bunch of clowns, themselves," he joked.

"Yes, well," flapped Mr. Kelly, towering over everybody like a tall skinny flagpole, "this library does seem to have become a bit of a circus. Perhaps you should go and mop the bathroom now, Frankie."

"On my way," said the caretaker airily.

"Thank you, Mr. Bela," I quavered after him as he left. He turned and gave a little bow.

"Call me Frankie, lovie," he said, and waved.

I called home, after that. Luckily, Dad was there, and he said he'd pick me up right away. I was so glad. It had been an awful day.

✿

In the morning I felt better, but Mom wouldn't let me take off the bandage. She wouldn't let me stay home from school, either, even though I begged and pleaded, and I knew she felt sorry for me, because she made me a special omelet for breakfast.

Dad felt sorry for me, too, and said he'd drive me to school. He'd been really angry when he arrived to pick me up at the library the night before.

"My daughter could have been seriously hurt," I heard him saying to Miss Spicer and Mr. Kelly, and they were apologizing over and over again. It was a bit unfair, really. My cut forehead wasn't their fault. It was the Phantom's.

"Maybe I shouldn't go to the library anymore," I said hopefully, at breakfast. If Mom and Dad banned me from going there, I wouldn't have to do the assignment. But unfortunately, Dad had calmed down quite a lot overnight.

"I don't think that's necessary, Richelle," he said. "Just take care."

My little brother Jason, who was staying home sick that day, lent me his lucky stone for the day. I guess having a cold made him forget he was a brat for a minute or two. But my older sister Tiffany thought the whole thing was very funny.

"You're the fashion queen, Richelle," she said nastily. "You might start a trend. Everyone will be wanting a bandage on their foreheads."

After that, I thought about cutting my hair so that it would cover my forehead. But I just couldn't bring myself to do it. I'd spent too long growing out my bangs. I tried tying a scarf around my head, but it didn't cover the bandage properly. I even thought about calling Sunny and asking to borrow one of her awful baseball caps. That's how desperate I was.

In the end, I wet my hair at the front, so it would lie flat across my forehead. If my hair's damp it just goes frizzy, so I was careful to comb a lot of water through it and really plaster it down. But of course plenty of people at school saw that stupid bandage anyway, and stared.

So I tried to make the most of a bad situation. At the end of our English lesson, I swept my hair off my forehead, and tried to get Mr. Raven to let me off doing the assignment. I said I'd been mentally scarred and was afraid to set foot in Raven Hill Library ever again. But it didn't work.

"All the more reason to go back, Richelle," he said earnestly. "You must fight your fear or you'll never get over it. And there's nothing to be afraid of, I'm sure. I'm positive that this Phantom person, whoever it is, didn't mean to hurt you."

So I used my other weapon. "There aren't any books about doughnuts in the library," I said.

"There is one," said Mr. Raven. "I came across it a few months ago."

"Well, what's it called?" I asked impatiently.

"I can't tell you that," he said. "It wouldn't be fair. You'll have to find it yourself."

I put on my most pleading expression. "I've typed all the words I can *think* of into that computer," I said. "I can't find *anything*."

He thought for a moment. "Listen carefully, Richelle," he said, pushing his glasses back on his nose. "If you need help, I won't *desert* you. I know you'll work the *whole* thing out." He smiled his dreadful smile at me. "There you are," he said triumphantly. "Now, off you go and think about that."

Think about what? He was crazy. He'd been no help at all.

7

Libraryphobia

So that afternoon, thanks to Mom, Dad, and Mr. Raven, I found myself walking with the others back to the library. I was in a very bad mood.

It was still raining. I'd forgotten my umbrella, and Elmo and I were both crammed under Liz's leaky red one with her. Elmo was droning on about how he couldn't stay long at the library because the *Pen* goes to print on Wednesday nights and he had to help. That boy thinks of nothing but the *Pen*. You'd think it was something really special, instead of just a little local newspaper.

I could feel cold drips running down the back of my neck and wriggled in annoyance, thinking about my hair and how frizzy it was probably getting.

We finally arrived at the library and I felt the familiar feeling of doom hit me as I walked through the foyer. I reached into my pocket. Jason's lucky stone felt cool and comforting in my hand. In the reading room, the others scattered in all directions, and I wandered toward the computer terminals.

I did a search using the word "snack," because that's what a doughnut is. But nothing came up. I tried "fat," because dough-nuts are fattening. But only diet books appeared on the screen.

Well, I'd tried my best. I'd just have to wait until I thought of another idea. In the meantime it was probably best to relax my brain by reading this fashion magazine I had in my bag.

I sat down in a chair attached to a desk near where Sunny was sitting. It was very uncomfortable not being able to move the chair closer to the desk. The others eventually came up, too, with their books. Everyone was working.

I stopped noticing their comings and goings after a while. I was doing this quiz: "Are you supermodel material?" Every question had three alternative answers: A, B, or C. I was concentrating hard because I wanted to get the highest score possible. So I didn't hear the soft footsteps behind me. And when someone lightly pulled my hair, I squeaked in fright.

I turned around and saw Frankie, the caretaker who had fixed my forehead, and Miss Spicer. They looked quite funny standing next to each other. Sort of cute. They were exactly the same size.

"Are you feeling better today, Richelle?" asked Miss Spicer. She was pale and she had shadows under her eyes, as if she hadn't slept well.

"Yes, thank you," I said politely.

"Mr. Kelly's feeling worse," joked Frankie. "It's his vanity. The lump on his head's gone down, but now he's got a huge purple bruise right in the middle of the bald spot." He laughed. "Like I told him, it's safer to keep your head where I do, closer to the ground."

I giggled. Frankie looked over my shoulder at the quiz I was reading. I hoped Miss Spicer wouldn't look as well. She'd be bound to disapprove.

"Is your assignment on the alphabet, like Elmo's?" asked Frankie, looking closely at the pages.

"Oh, no, this isn't for my assignment," I said, knowing I'd probably turned bright red. "I just . . . um . . . thought I'd look at this magazine for a minute. You know, just to take a break." I thought it was a bit mean of Frankie to make fun of me in front of Miss Spicer.

Miss Spicer sighed, but didn't say anything. She patted me on the shoulder and the two of them walked away, talking quietly to each other, as Liz and Nick came back to our table. Tom, I saw, had been with them, but was now lurking behind a shelf, watching Miss Spicer's retreating back.

"We're going to borrow some books and take them home, Richelle," Liz said. "Do you want to leave soon? It's nearly four-thirty."

I nodded and started putting my magazine back in my bag.

Liz looked at the magazine, and at my empty desk. "Haven't you started yet?" she asked. "You'd better get a move on. It's already Wednesday afternoon."

"I know what day it is," I snapped at her. "The book I need isn't here at the moment, that's all."

"I wish I had that problem," groaned Nick. "I don't know why I chose *R* for Rats. I must have been insane. I hate rats and mice."

I do, too. I hate their beady little eyes and slimy tails. I didn't envy Nick one little bit.

"Murophobia," hissed Tom, emerging suddenly from his hiding place.

"What?" I exploded.

"Fear of rats and mice," he said knowledgeably.

"Why is Elmo still here?" asked Nick suddenly, changing the subject. Maybe he thought it hadn't been cool to admit that he hated rats.

"He says he has a hunch that something else is going to happen," said Tom. "He's after a last-minute scoop for the *Pen*."

He sat down on a table. I noticed that he was carrying his bag. "Are you leaving, too, Tom?" I asked, not very enthusiastically. When I go down a street with Tom, somehow I always end up being totally embarrassed, or covered with food, or something. He's like a walking disaster waiting to happen.

He scrunched up his face. "I have to," he said. "It's too quiet here. My iPod needs to be recharged, and I can't work without music. In other words, I do *not* have acousticophobia."

He waited for someone to ask what that was. No one did.

"Fear of noise," he explained, anyway. "But I can't borrow anything to take home until I return the book I've got. So I'm going home to find it once and for all!"

He yelled out the last words like a hero from an adventure movie. An old lady reading the paper nearby looked up crossly.

"Let's go then," I said quickly, and started to hustle them all toward the door before he could get us into any more trouble. We passed the shelves. We passed the computer terminals. We waved to Sunny, who was still working, and to Elmo, who was still prowling around with his camera.

We almost made it out. But we weren't fast enough. Liz and Nick stopped to borrow their books at the desk. And then we heard a loud bang and a bloodcurdling yell. The Phantom had found another target.

8

Page one

A plump man came storming from the direction of the men's room, trailing a cloud of white dust and quivering with fury. His stylish pin-striped suit was almost completely covered in white. White powder also clung to his cellphone, his briefcase, his shiny bald head, and his face. He rubbed his eyes furiously with one pudgy hand and shook a book in the air with the other.

"What on earth is going on here?" he yelled, marching up to us, leaving white footprints behind him. Miss Spicer and Mr. Kelly gaped at him from across the counter of the borrowing desk.

The man slammed the book onto the desk.

"What sort of place are you running here?" he yelled, as people started crowding around. "A bag fell on my head when I walked into the men's restroom. What is this? And this?" He stabbed a blunt finger first at the powder and then at the book.

"Looks like flour," murmured Elmo, taking photos like crazy. "And a copy of *Hamlet*."

"Mommy, that man looks like a ghost," I heard a little girl say.

Miss Spicer heard, too, and looked unhappily at the man. "I'm very sorry, sir," she whispered. "I think it's supposed to be a . . . a joke. Relating to the ghost in *Hamlet*."

"What?" I whispered to Liz.

"Don't know," she whispered back. "*Hamlet*'s a play by Shakespeare, but I haven't read it."

"Look," Miss Spicer went on, trying to smile. "Here comes Frankie with some tissues for you, sir. And if you'll send us your dry-cleaning bill, we'll be happy to pay —"

"You bet you will!" growled the man, and he stormed out without waiting for Frankie or the tissues or anything else.

We left, too. Elmo walked with us just long enough to tell us that in *Hamlet* the main character, Prince Hamlet, keeps seeing the ghost of his murdered father. Then he bolted off to the *Pen*, splashing through puddles and looking very pleased with himself.

✿

The next morning, Thursday, we had to deliver the *Pen* as usual. The plump businessman (who turned out to be Rupert Molly, one of the local bank managers) had made the front page. And to my horror, I had, too. Elmo's photo of Mr. Molly had been enlarged. It was an amazing photo. Even I had to admit that. You could actually see the flour flying out of the man's mouth as he yelled.

The photo of me, pale and huddled on a chair in the library, was smaller and farther down the page. But it was still very embarrassing, especially because I had to deliver some of the papers myself.

Zim handed us our bundles of papers and smiled at me. "Exciting, isn't it?" he said, pointing to my photo. Exciting wasn't the word I'd use. I thought that it would be rude to complain to Zim about the story, so I complained to Elmo instead.

"Where's your loyalty? And why give this stupid Phantom free publicity?" I hissed in his ear.

He shrugged. "Bad news is good news," he said. Elmo says that a lot. It means that people are more interested in reading about disasters and crime than nice, happy news. Well, I'd always agreed in the past, but it was different when it was your own personal disaster plastered across the front page.

For once, I went home for breakfast. I didn't feel like hanging around with the others. But I should have stayed away. My family had seen the *Pen*.

"That guy from the bank looks like such a dork," said Tiff, snickering at the photographs. "You look almost dignified in comparison, Richelle."

"That was a very, very dangerous and stupid trick," muttered Dad, chewing his way mournfully through the cereal he called "chicken feed." "I knew someone who was nearly blinded by a flour bomb. People don't realize —"

"Lucky you had my stone, Richelle," croaked Jason hoarsely, "or you could've been hurt again. The Phantom's probably booby-trapped the entire library."

"I don't want to go there anymore!" I cried miserably. My bottom lip started to quiver, and I felt my eyes filling with tears. Tiff looked at me disgustedly. She thought I was acting, which was very unfair because I wasn't. Though I must admit I didn't exactly try to *stop* the tears, either.

Mom hesitated, and glanced at Dad. They'd obviously talked about this. "You've got dance class this afternoon, so you can't go today, anyway, darling. We'll discuss the whole thing tonight," she said.

○

It rained all that morning. It rained all through lunch.

By the time we got to English, the last class of the day on Thursdays, the thunder and lightning had started all over again. I was the last person to come in, and the only desk left was right up at the front under Mr. Raven's beaky nose.

He wrote a lot of stuff on the blackboard about the book we were reading and tried to start a discussion. But no one was really enthusiastic. Liz and Elmo ended up answering most of the questions.

At the end of the class, he suddenly asked how our assignments were going. Everyone sort of nodded unhappily, or quietly said, "Good," or something like that.

Mr. Raven looked disappointed. "Aren't you enjoying the assignment?" he asked. His pale green eyes stared at us from behind the thick black frames of his glasses.

"It's . . . um . . . it's not that," stammered Liz. "It's just . . . um . . . the weather. It's depressing, that's all."

"Strange — I quite like it," muttered Mr. Raven to himself, watching the lightning flash outside. He spun around suddenly to face us again.

"Is it the library that's the problem?" he asked, almost eagerly. "Do the Phantom's jokes scare you?"

"What, are we in kindergarten now?" muttered Nick from somewhere behind me. But no one else said anything.

"There's really nothing to fear," said Mr. Raven in his monotonous voice. "Nothing at all. I worked at the library for years, and there was never any danger."

"Well, that was before buckets started falling on people's heads," said Sunny flatly.

I crossed my fingers. With any luck, Raven Mad would call the whole project off, and I'd be saved.

But he did no such thing. "It's unfortunate," he commented, his bony fingers fidgeting rather unpleasantly on the desk. He seemed to be thinking about something other than the assignment, that was for sure.

The bell rang, and he looked up. His fingers stopped moving. "Who here knows what a group of ravens is called?" he asked drearily.

Nobody did.

"It's called an 'unkindness' of ravens," he said, with a ghost of a smile. "An unkindness."

"Well, there's the word of the day," said Tom out of the corner of his mouth. It was the first time he'd spoken all class.

Everyone picked up their bags and slunk miserably out of the room. When I looked back through the window, Mr. Raven was still hunched over the desk. Lightning flashed on his glasses, and his bloodless lips murmured words that only he could hear.

An unkindness of ravens. How depressing. Now I understood the name of his painting. That was depressing, too.

We all said good-bye, and then I left for dance class. It turned out no one was going to the library that afternoon, anyway. My dance class was okay, but my heart really wasn't in it.

The dance room has these huge mirrors, so you can watch yourself moving. I usually like it. But today, the mirrors reflected not just us, but also the storm that was going on outside the old windows. And in my head I kept seeing Mr. Raven's strange smile, and the awful image of an unkindness of ravens perched spookily in the library attic.

9

Gossip

Friday arrived in a flash of lightning and a clap of thunder. This weather was getting ridiculous. The only good thing was that I could finally take the bandage off my forehead.

Unfortunately for me, Mom and Dad had worked out a plan so that I could avoid spending much time in the library, but could still do my assignment. Mom was going to lend me her library card so I could borrow the books I needed and work on my report at home. Little did they know that in all this time I hadn't found any books to work with. And I didn't dare tell them.

Jason was still officially sick, although I could see he was much better because he was back to his usual obnoxious self. When he's really sick, he becomes quite peaceful and lovable.

"There's a trip to the library today, but I don't have to go," he jeered. "You do, Richelle! Hahaha!"

"Can I keep the lucky stone for another day?" I asked, and he graciously gave me permission.

I heard that annoying laugh in my head again as I walked into school. I wished for a really bad cold to strike me down, anything so that I could go home instead of to the library. Luckily we had assembly in the morning, and we missed out on English.

"Thank goodness," I sighed to Liz as we sat down in the school hall. "I really couldn't take Mr. Raven today."

"Come on, Richelle. He's not that bad," said Liz. "He's got a good imagination."

"Well, he stinks as a teacher," I said. "He's so . . . so *weird*. His eyes are pale and spooky. And his fingers are so long and bony."

"Richelle, don't judge a book by its cover. He can't help the way he looks," scolded Liz.

There was that phrase again. I knew I wasn't going to win this argument. Liz always feels sorry for the kind of people who I don't like.

○

Liz and Sunny didn't go to the library that afternoon, so I had to walk there listening to Tom and Nick picking on each other the whole way. Elmo was thinking about something or other, so he wasn't any help. I guessed that Tom hadn't found his overdue book, because he recharged his iPod on the way.

"You can't keep out of Spicer's way forever, Moysten," taunted Nick.

"Why are you here?" I asked him. "You borrowed books the other day, like Liz, didn't you?"

Nick fell silent for a minute. "I've finished with those books," he said finally.

"But you can keep books for a week," I said. "You don't have to return them right away."

Nick said nothing, and shrugged awkwardly.

"Can't stand to have all those mousy pictures lying around your room, can you, murophobe?" snickered Tom.

Nick scowled, but Tom grinned at me.

"Nick had this dream last night that there was a huge mouse with red eyes looking in through his window, didn't you, Nickie?" he teased.

"I never should have told you about that, Moysten," growled Nick. He glanced at Elmo, who was looking at him sideways. "Well, it was a scary dream," he said, defending himself.

I could just imagine. I shivered.

"Nickory Dickory Dock," sang Tom,

"The mouse ran up the clock,

The clock struck one,

Nick's assignment's not done,

Nickory Dickory Dock!"

"Well, my project isn't done, either," said Elmo.

"And I haven't seen your assignment neatly written out and ready, Moysten!" said Nick.

"Well, of course not!" said Tom, acting surprised at the suggestion. "What's a project about phobias without an interview with Nick-murophobe-Kontellis!"

Nick kicked the puddles.

"Stupid rats. Stupid library," he grumbled. "Stupid Raven."

"He'll be here this afternoon," said Elmo. We stopped and stared at him.

"What, to spy on us?" I asked wildly.

"No, no," laughed Elmo. "I saw him this afternoon. He said he'd come to find a book I need. It's marked 'out for repair' on the catalog, but he said he knew where it was. He was in charge of repairing the books when he worked at the library."

"And how is old Raven Mad?" Tom inquired. "Mad as ever?"

Elmo frowned. "No," he said. "He seemed kind of sad. Or bored. Or angry, or something."

The library loomed ahead of us. Two women were standing on the steps, talking. "Oh, no," I said suddenly, as one of the women began waving to me vigorously. "It's Mrs. Bradshaw."

"Who?" said Tom, peering around me to see.

"A friend of Mom's," I explained, looking around desperately for some way to escape. But it was too late. My so-called friends zipped past me and into the library as Mrs. Bradshaw pounced.

"Hello, Richelle dear," she said, with a bright pink-lipsticked smile. It clashed with her red raincoat, I noticed. "Do you remember Mrs. Collins?"

The other lady smiled, showing perfect white teeth. "My son Peter is friends with your little brother," she explained.

"And how is Jason? Not too sick I hope?" asked Mrs. Bradshaw. Her son Mark was in Jason's class, too.

"Just a cold," I said. "Are you waiting to pick up Mark and Peter from the library trip?"

They shook their heads.

"We kept them home today," explained Mrs. Bradshaw. "The library is too dangerous for children at the moment."

"We came down to talk to their teacher about our concern," said Mrs. Collins. "We really think the trip should have been canceled."

Mrs. Bradshaw lowered her voice. "Mr. Kelly came out and spoke to us a few minutes ago," she said. "Apparently, the police were at the library this morning. Testing the men's bathroom for fingerprints. Mr. Molly made a big fuss. Quite justifiably."

"Mr. Molly?" I asked vaguely.

"The man from the bank who was hit by the flour yesterday." Mrs. Bradshaw nodded seriously.

"There were no fingerprints in the bathroom, unfortunately," said Mrs. Collins. "That funny little caretaker man had cleaned it. Well, I suppose he had to. Apparently, there was flour everywhere."

"I'm very sorry for Miss Spicer," Mrs. Bradshaw went on, not looking sorry at all, "but I really do agree she isn't handling this problem well. Apparently, the supervisor is very concerned. The library has insurance, but that's not the point."

"Don't forget the *Pen*," Mrs. Collins reminded her. "It's been very irresponsible, too. People are saying it's been encouraging this Phantom, you know, by giving him a nickname and so much publicity."

"What people?" I asked. "Who's saying this?"

"Everyone," said Mrs. Collins vaguely. "Everyone's talking about it."

Mrs. Bradshaw's eyes narrowed. "Does your mother know you're here?" she asked me suspiciously.

"Oh, yes," I said. "I'm not staying long. I just have to borrow a book. Well, see you later."

I smiled as charmingly as I could and made my escape.

"Ask Delia to give me a call, will you, Richelle?" Mrs. Bradshaw called after me. "And you just be careful in there."

I waved and walked on, thinking how strange it was that the library could suddenly turn into a place that people thought of as dangerous. It seemed ridiculous.

But it was true. And it was going to get worse.

10

Bleak House

As soon as I got inside, I ducked into the ladies' room to tie back my hair. The chat with Mrs. Bradshaw in the drizzle had turned it into one enormous frizzy bunch of knots. When I came out, I saw Nick at the borrowing desk, returning the books he'd borrowed to Mr. Kelly.

I bit my lip to keep myself from giggling. Mr. Kelly was trying to look as dignified as usual, but he looked really silly. The bruise on his head was purple and green now, and the long hair around his bald patch frizzed and stuck out at all kinds of odd angles. His chat with Mrs. Bradshaw in the rain obviously hadn't agreed with his hair, either.

"Isn't it quiet?" said Nick suddenly, as we walked back toward the computer terminals.

"It's a library. Of course it's quiet," I snapped, noticing with annoyance that his hair was as smooth as ever.

"It's not the normal kind of quiet," he persisted.

I realized he was right. In the reading corner Miss Spicer was just finishing talking to a group of kids from Jason's class, but there were only about six of them there. I guess a lot of other parents besides Mrs. Collins and Mrs. Bradshaw were taking the Phantom danger seriously.

Mr. Kelly was at the borrowing desk. Frankie, looking rather depressed, was watering the potted plants. But there were no other staff around at all. The other staff were part-time, I remembered. They'd probably been sent home. There were hardly any visitors to help, so they weren't needed.

As we watched, the kids all got up and were ushered out by their teacher. After that, the place was practically deserted. There were just a few people looking around cautiously as they hurried among the shelves.

The quiet was uneasy. It was spooky.

Tom and Elmo came up to us, and I told Elmo what Mrs. Bradshaw had said.

"That's ridiculous," he growled. "It's not the *Pen*'s fault that the Phantom decided to turn nasty. Or Miss Spicer's."

"Maybe if she hadn't encouraged the jokes, things wouldn't have gone so far," I suggested.

But Elmo shook his head violently. "Miss Spicer thought she was helping the library. The Phantom jokes made people come here more often. But it's all gone sour." He looked around, frowning. "People only blame Miss Spicer and the *Pen* because they don't know who the Phantom is," he said slowly. "He must be someone who's in the library often. If only we could find out. . . ."

His voice trailed off, and he and Nick exchanged glances. I felt a prickle of panic. I knew what that look meant.

I zipped across to the computer terminals before they could suggest anything I didn't want to hear. I typed in "jam" and "cinnamon," but nothing useful came up. I stamped my foot in irritation.

"Stupid assignment," I said crossly, walking back to the others.

"Watch what you say," muttered Nick smoothly, nodding his head in the direction of the borrowing desk. I turned to look. Mr. Raven had come in and was standing there, talking to Miss Spicer seriously. She looked very tired and depressed. Mr. Raven pointed to the storeroom behind the stairs and said something, and she shook her head and replied, handing him a key.

"Maybe he thinks she's put his 'Unkindness' painting in the storeroom," I whispered.

"Actually, Richelle, he's saying. 'I think I might have left my alphabet undies in the storeroom. Have you seen them?'" said Tom, pretending to lip-read. "And she's saying, 'No, but here's the key, you can have a look if you like.'"

"*Tom!*" I hissed, scandalized that he could even think of a teacher and his underwear. Especially a teacher like Mr. Raven.

"For sure he's just asking about that book I wanted," said Elmo calmly. "Look, he's going to check it out."

Mr. Raven was turning the key in the door of the storeroom. Then he pulled the door open. And then he gasped.

"Mary!" he almost screamed to Miss Spicer.

Miss Spicer, Mr. Kelly, and every other person in the library, including us, froze for a moment, then raced to crowd around the storeroom door. My heart was beating quickly. What had Mr. Raven seen? A ghost? A dead body?

But it wasn't anything like that. There were tall shelves in the room, piled high with boxes, books, and all sorts of things. But the floor was covered with masses of papers — you could have swum in them. And the papers were the pages of books that someone had ripped to pieces. . . .

Miss Spicer was crying. She was kneeling down, picking up one page after another from the mess. "Wicked," she was sobbing.

Then she shrieked. She'd uncovered a mousetrap, complete with a dead mouse.

"Oh, dear," muttered Frankie. "There were a couple of traps in here. I didn't have a chance to check them this morning." He bent and wrapped the trap, and the mouse, in an old plastic bag. Then he just stood there, holding the bag in his hand.

Nick and I shuddered.

Something was taped to the inside of the storeroom door — the cover of a book from which all the pages had been ripped. Mr. Raven pulled the cover off. He handed it to Miss Spicer with trembling hands.

She gasped. "My copy of *Bleak House*," she whispered. "This is a very early edition. It's been in my family for years. I gave it to the library."

She pressed her fingers over her lips and stared at the empty cover. Frankie breathed in sharply and bent toward her.

"This isn't the book you told me about, is it?" he asked her. "Your favorite, the one by Charles Dickens, with all the wonderful characters? And the court case?"

"Yes," said Miss Spicer with tears in her eyes.

She got up and backed out of the storeroom, holding the

cover in her hand. Wiping her eyes, she looked around at the small group of people in front of her, at the empty library beyond, then back at the ruined books in the storeroom.

"I suppose this 'house' has become rather 'bleak,' lately, hasn't it?" murmured Mr. Raven.

No one said anything. Mr. Kelly sighed deeply and ran his hand through his hair. Frankie nervously tapped the plastic bag containing the dead mouse with his fingertips.

"The mouse has become rather bleak as well," joked Tom weakly, to fill the silence. "It's a bleak mouse."

Nick and I shuddered.

"Murophobes!" said Tom, determined to make us smile.

Miss Spicer laughed, but not pleasantly, and her little black eyes flashed angrily. "This is no joke," she said loudly. "This is wicked destruction. And when" — her voice rose and rose to an angry squeak — "when I find out who did it, they're going to pay — very dearly!"

11

Blame

Miss Spicer went over to the borrowing desk and shoved the empty cover into one of the drawers.

"Are you all right, Mary?" said Frankie. He took her hand, looking very worried.

"Mary," said Mr. Kelly in a deep, serious voice. "All this has got to stop." He was standing over her, looking down at her from his great height, and she seemed to shrink.

"I've held my tongue for a month," he went on. "But —"

"You haven't held your tongue, you skinny tent-pole," roared Frankie suddenly. "You've flapped it till we're all sick of it, and you're flapping it now!"

Mr. Kelly turned a dull red that clashed horribly with his hair.

"You just leave Mary alone!" yelled Frankie. "She's doing her best. She's worked in this place for thirty years! I've been here for only two of them. But I know there's no one who loves this library like she does."

"That's right," said Elmo loudly. And a few people echoed him.

Mr. Kelly, his mustache bristling, shook a trembling finger in Elmo's face.

"You're partly to blame for this, Alvin," he shouted. "That newspaper of your father's has glorified this Phantom. Encouraged these stupid, so-called jokes . . ."

"My name's Elmo!" Elmo snapped. "And you can't blame the *Pen* for —"

"I can, and I do!" Mr. Kelly roared back. "I am going to write to the local Press Council and complain about you. Taking photographs without permission, encouraging vandalism, creating a climate of panic . . ."

"That's completely unfair!" Elmo was really angry now. He's usually so quiet, but when he loses his temper, he really loses it. And I think he'd defend the *Pen* with the last drop of his blood.

I can't stand scenes. Usually, I try to get as far away from them as possible. But Elmo was getting more furious every second and making everything worse. Tom and Nick were already moving up beside him, muttering in his ear. I knew that if Sunny and Liz had been there, they would have, too. Although I didn't want to, I had to stick around.

I couldn't comfort Elmo, like Liz would have done. I never know what to say. I couldn't make jokes to make him calm down, like Tom was trying to do. I can never remember jokes. I couldn't reason with him, like Nick. He wouldn't listen to me. And I couldn't face up to Mr. Kelly, all calm and strong, like Sunny would have done.

But charming adults into doing what you want — now *that* I understand. I went and stood between Mr. Kelly and the others, and looked up at him.

I opened my big blue eyes wide and willed them to fill with tears. "Elmo and his dad really love this library, Mr. Kelly. They'd *never* encourage violence here on purpose," I said, in my softest, sweetest voice, with just a little tremble in it.

He started to look a little uncertain. Some of the angry red went out of his face.

"When the Phantom jokes started, they did seem like fun," I whispered, biting my lip and looking up at him. "It's just so . . . so awful, that it's ended up like this." I let a tear spill over and roll down my cheek.

"Go, Richelle," Tom muttered under his breath, behind me. The idiot!

But Mr. Kelly hadn't heard. He was really softening up now and getting more and more embarrassed. After all, people were watching. He ran his hand over his bald patch. "Now, now," he said. "No need to get upset."

He cleared his throat and looked over my shoulder at Elmo. "I'm sorry . . . ah . . . Elmo," he said. "It was wrong of me to blame you — or the *Pen*. I'm just very tense about all this. I apologize."

Elmo nodded, his face still very serious.

"I'm calling the police again," said Miss Spicer, in a quavering voice. She reached for the telephone.

❄

Two police officers arrived quite quickly. They checked out the storeroom, then went right around the whole building.

They asked Mr. Kelly, Miss Spicer, and Frankie when they

had last visited the storeroom. None of them had been in it all day, though Frankie had visited it the day before.

"Obviously, the damage was done last night, when the library was closed," said Miss Spicer, rather impatiently.

"Like most of the other tricks," said one of the police, a big, freckled man called Officer Klein.

"But there's no sign of a break-in, is there?" commented his partner, a nice woman named Officer Greta Vortek, whom we'd met a few times before. "The offender must have hidden in the library after closing."

"Impossible!" snapped Mr. Kelly. "I was the last to leave and I checked every possible hiding place. I've taken to doing that since this Phantom thing first came to my attention. There was definitely no one here last night."

"Then the offender must have had a key," Greta said.

Mr. Kelly shook his head. His wild, frizzy bangs and bruised bald spot made him look like a clown. "Only Miss Spicer, Frankie, and I have keys," he said. "So that can't be it."

Miss Spicer made a small, protesting sound, as if she was about to say something, then looked flustered.

The two police exchanged glances.

"Did you have anything to add to that, Miss Spicer?" Officer Klein asked politely.

Miss Spicer looked confused. "Well no . . . yes . . ." she said. "Just that . . . I have misplaced my keys a few times over the past months. . . ."

"A *few* times?" I heard Mr. Kelly mutter to Mr. Raven. "She's *always* leaving them around."

"You're suggesting someone could have taken the keys and had copies made of them?" Officer Klein said.

Miss Spicer nodded miserably. "It's possible," she said, looking at the floor. "Though I don't think —"

"What?" urged Greta, leaning forward.

"I don't think a member of the public could have taken them," she whispered. "I never have my keys with me in the reading room or the attic. Only in the staff-only areas."

The police exchanged glances again. Then Greta turned to us. "Do you have anything to add to any of this?" she asked.

We shook our heads.

"But Help-for-Hire Inc. loves solving mysteries," she said teasingly. "I'd have thought you'd have the Phantom unmasked by now."

We all laughed politely. Greta and Officer Klein put away their notebooks, thanked everyone for their time, and left. Nick and Elmo went with them.

"Where are *they* going?" I said to Tom crossly.

"Trying to find out who the cops suspect, of course," he hissed back. Then he stared at me. "Look, Richelle, don't you understand? Hey, wake up. The Phantom got into the building last night with a key. Only the library staff *have* keys — or the chance to copy Miss Spicer's. So . . ."

"The Phantom is one of them," I whispered, suddenly understanding. "A staff member. I can't believe it."

"You've got no choice," he said grimly.

I thought for a moment, and I could see he was right. "But, Tom —" I whispered. "Which one is it?"

He looked worried. "That's what we'd all like to know," he said.

✿

Nick and Elmo came back and said that as far as they could tell the police had no firm suspect, though they were now certain that the Phantom was a member of the library staff — temporary or permanent.

"I'd say they're just waiting for the next Phantom trick to happen," Nick said in a low voice. "They say they're understaffed themselves. They can't stake out the library twenty-four hours a day."

Miss Spicer sat at the borrowing desk, twisting strands of her hair around her fingers. Frankie watched her worriedly. Mr. Raven hung around, looking miserable.

"I think we should close the library over the weekend," Mr. Kelly suggested briskly. "We'll clean up the storeroom, get rid of the rubbish, and —"

"No!" said Miss Spicer. She let go of her hair and clenched her fists. "The library must stay open. We'll hire a team to spend Saturday collecting the pages of every book into a separate box. We'll use the emergency cash fund."

"It's not worth it!" exclaimed Mr. Kelly. But Miss Spicer hardly seemed to hear him.

"We need to try to save as many of those books as we can. It wasn't just my copy of *Bleak House* that was rare. Isn't that right, Mark?" she said, appealing to Mr. Raven.

"Oh, absolutely," said Mr. Raven, looking doubtfully at the mess of pages in the storeroom.

That was when Nick pulled us all aside. "Listen," he said quickly and quietly. "How about Help-for-Hire Inc. offers to take the job?"

"Isn't that like making a profit out of their disaster?" Elmo objected.

"As you know, I have ergophobia — an intense fear of work — but I could use the money," said Tom. "And old Spicer's so worried she's not going to give me a hard time about that lost book."

I thought about it. Maybe if I was helping Mr. Raven's beloved library, he'd give me an extension on my project out of gratitude.

"It would be nice to help out," I said sweetly. They all looked at me in amazement. I don't usually volunteer for work.

But Nick wasn't finished.

"It's not just because of the helping. Or the money," he whispered. "I was thinking of another reason why it would be good to be on the scene."

I shook my head violently. "*No!*" I said through gritted teeth. "Just *forget* it!"

"Forget what?" asked Tom, confused.

"Nick's going to suggest that we should take this job so that we can find out who the Phantom is," I whispered angrily.

"Great idea!" said Elmo.

"No it *isn't!*" I hissed. "We'll just get ourselves into trouble again, like we always do."

"Richelle, all I'm suggesting is that we keep our eyes open," said Nick. "It's worked for us before."

"It's not really our business," muttered Tom.

"Of *course* it's our business," Elmo said. "Richelle's been hurt, Dad and I have been blamed, and no one in Raven Hill feels safe enough to come to the library anymore."

Tom shrugged and nodded. Then Nick called Liz and Sunny, and they both agreed as well. So I was outnumbered. I gave in and said I'd be in it, too, as long as I didn't have to snoop around. *After all*, I thought, *I did want to get Mr. Raven on my side.*

But Mr. Raven was with Miss Spicer when Elmo asked her if we could have the job. And just after she'd smiled and said yes, yes, of course we could, Mr. Raven smiled his own ghostly smile and murmured: "As long as this doesn't interfere with your assignments."

"Oh, it won't," Nick assured him. "We've got time to do both."

So much for my idea. As we left, I felt like a deflated balloon. I still had an assignment due on Monday. And now I had to spend the weekend in the library. With the Phantom.

12

Piece by piece

On Saturday morning I arrived at the library at about the same time all the others did, thanks to Dad giving me a lift.

"On time, Richelle. A record!" Liz teased as we walked up the steps in the rain, carrying the shoe boxes we'd all brought with us to help us sort the books.

"If you don't stop hassling Richelle about being late, she'll develop chronomeatrophobia — fear of clocks," said Tom proudly. "To go with her rhytiphobia."

"What's that?" I snapped. I had to know.

"Fear of getting wrinkles," he sighed happily. He'd been dying for me to ask.

I pushed the doors and they creaked open. Miss Spicer had left them unlocked for us, thank goodness.

Inside, the building was very, very quiet. And still. And there was something else. Something in the air, like fear, or a threat. I'm very sensitive to things like that. It felt awful. Tom shivered.

"Something's not right," he said. "I feel it in my bones." His voice sounded hollow in the dim foyer.

"Well, at least you have a feeling somewhere other than in your stomach for a change, Moysten," teased Nick.

"Don't joke about it, Nick," I whispered. "This place is so creepy."

"You guys are just letting yourself be spooked by the Phantom like everyone else," said Nick loudly as we walked into the main part of the library. Liz shushed him, but he waved at her irritably. "He's just some pathetic little loser with a major need for attention," he went on. "Wait till we find out who he is."

"Nick!" hissed Liz, and Sunny poked him in the ribs. Then he realized why they were trying to make him be quiet. We weren't alone. Miss Spicer, Mr. Kelly, Mr. Raven, and Frankie were standing near the borrowing desk, staring at us. They'd obviously heard every word Nick had said.

"Out to catch the Phantom, kids?" asked Frankie.

Nick said nothing, but his ears were pink with embarrassment.

"It beats catching mice, anyway," joked Tom. "How big was the one in the mousetrap yesterday, Frankie?"

"Huge!" said Frankie.

"Nibbly little teeth, shiny little claws . . ." snickered Tom. He glanced slyly at Nick, who was now looking a bit pale. I didn't feel too comfortable myself.

"Well, then," said Miss Spicer, a little flustered, "I'll just show you to the storeroom. . . ."

Mr. Raven and Mr. Kelly nodded to us as we passed them. Mr. Raven looked as pale as a ghost, with deep gray shadows under his eyes. Mr. Kelly looked more normal. The bruise on his head had faded to light brown, and his hair was only a bit frizzy. He must have worn a hat to work.

Miss Spicer unlocked the storeroom door and turned on the lights. We all filed in, shuffling through the sea of paper on the floor.

The room was chilly and dull. It was long and narrow. Tall shelves lined the walls. Next to the door was a small desk.

"Mark Raven kept a record of all the books that came in to be repaired," said Miss Spicer. "And no books have been put in here since he left."

She picked up a thick, red book from the desk. "He'd tick off each book when it was ready to be put back on the shelves. See?" She pointed to the well-organized pages, with their perfectly ruled margins and incredibly neat handwriting.

"Oh, that'll help a lot," said Liz. "It's lucky *this* book wasn't damaged."

"Mark did do a good job," said Miss Spicer primly.

"A shame that he left, in that case," observed Liz.

"Yes," said Miss Spicer. "He really seemed to belong here."

Well, that said it all about Mr. Raven, in my opinion. Anyone who belonged to a horrible little room like this just had to be strange.

"But when our budget was cut, we couldn't afford all the part-time workers anymore," Miss Spicer continued. "Mark was good with the books — but not so happy dealing with people, if you know what I mean. So he was the one who had to go." It was hard to tell exactly how she felt about that.

After she'd gone we just stood there, staring at the mess.

"According to this, there were twenty books left in here," said Liz, closing the record book.

"Imagine spending hours and hours a week in this room," said Sunny. "I don't know how Mr. Raven could stand it."

Tom started talking about his claustrophobia — fear of enclosed spaces — but I stopped listening. I'd suddenly had a flash of memory. It was Mr. Raven, talking to me in the staffroom. He'd said he knew there was a library book with information on doughnuts because he'd come across it himself.

Maybe he'd repaired it! I got the record book from Liz and flipped back through the pages. And there it was. *The A–Z of Desserts*.

Of course! I'd been so stupid! When Mr. Raven had said "I won't desert you" he'd been giving me a clue! He'd been trying to tell me to enter "dessert" into the computer.

As soon as we take a break, I'll go out and look up *The A–Z of Desserts*, I promised myself. I felt so relieved. I was going to get my assignment done on time after all.

"I can't believe all this paper came out of only twenty books," grumbled Nick, kicking at the pages on the floor.

"Let's just get started," said Sunny. "The more we stand and stare at this, the harder it's going to seem."

Between us we had sixteen shoe boxes, and we found four more empty boxes on the storeroom shelves. We labeled each box with the title of one of the twenty books in Mr. Raven's record. And then we began.

It was actually sort of fun. We found the covers first and put them in their boxes. Most of them still had a few pages hanging on inside. We found them all except *Bleak House*. It was probably still in the borrowing desk drawer. Then we started sorting through the loose pages, finding the ones that matched each book.

Sometimes the name of the book was printed on the top of every page, or it was obvious from the words on the page where it belonged. But when that didn't happen, it was harder. You had to look for clues in the printing, the size of the pages, or the paper.

I was quite good at that. People often tell me I have a good eye for detail. Elmo was good at it, too. But he kept reading the pages that he was supposed to be sorting.

Tom was hopeless, and Nick wasn't much better.

"Look, I'm telling you, Kontellis," Tom said. "These pages are *definitely* from the same book."

"They can't be, Moysten you idiot," argued Nick. "Look at these page numbers. They're both page forty! It's impossible."

"It's possible!" Tom argued back. "A misprint . . . a mistake . . . an amazing new concept in page numbering . . ."

"Try again, Moysten," growled Nick.

Tom looked helplessly at the pages in his hand.

"Oh, really," I said in annoyance, taking them from him. "Look! Can't you see that the paper is different? This one's thicker and a bit yellower. It belongs to Elmo's alphabet book. The other one is finer. It's probably — yes, look. It matches the pages in the *Bleak House* box."

I put the pages in their proper places. They looked at me in disbelief. I was pleased. It was good to be an expert.

"Poor Miss Spicer must have been upset about her *Bleak House*," sighed Liz. "I really wish we could find out who the Phantom is."

"Well, that's what we're here for," said Nick, and my heart sank.

"It's obviously someone with a secret grudge against books, or the library," Liz went on. "They started off with funny little jokes, then once they'd gotten everyone interested, they moved on to nastier and nastier ones, so everyone would be scared."

"We know it's one of the library staff, right?" said Elmo. "It's just a question of working out which one. There are three temporary staff —"

"Four counting Raven Mad," said Tom. "He only stopped working here a few weeks ago."

Elmo nodded. "Okay," he said. "Four temporary staff, plus Miss Spicer, Mr. Kelly, and Frankie. Seven people to choose from."

"It can't be Kelly," said Nick. "Don't you remember? He was on vacation when the Phantom jokes started."

"It can't be Frankie," I put in, despite the fact that I'd been determined not to play any part in this. "He doesn't have any reason to hate books or the library."

"Well, it can't be Miss Spicer, either," said Elmo. "She *loves* books and the library."

"And it can't be Mr. Raven," said Liz. "He does, too. Look at the way this record's set out. And he's written in a special fountain pen, not just an ordinary pen. This job was special to him. It looks like he really enjoyed it."

Tom shrugged. "Simple, then," he said. "It must be one of the other three temp workers."

"It's hard to believe. They just seem like ordinary, nice women," Liz said, and Elmo nodded in agreement.

I went back to sorting pages. All this talk was getting us nowhere, and that suited me fine.

Elmo had been thinking. "Maybe we're going about this the wrong way," he said. "Maybe instead of just guessing about who the Phantom is, we should be looking for evidence."

"There must be clues around the library somewhere," agreed Tom. "A lot of the jokes have been done in a hurry."

Liz looked up. "Hey, you know, if I was the Phantom," she said slowly, "maybe I'd think this storeroom was a really good place to hide things."

"Maybe you're right," said Nick. He stood up, and started prowling around. Elmo joined him, looking carefully behind boxes and all the other stacked-up junk.

I kept working. I didn't want any part of this. But I looked up like everyone else when Elmo gave a gasp. He pulled out a plain white plastic bag from behind a box on the very bottom shelf in the corner.

We all got up and crowded around him as he rummaged through the bag.

"A few old chocolate frogs, half a packet of red stickers, play money . . . and an empty pack of flour," he said excitedly.

"No way!" said Tom, just as excited. "Hey! We've found the Phantom's bag of tricks!"

13

A nasty shock

Elmo cleared a space on the carpet and emptied out the bag. As well as the other things he'd told us about, there was a folded sheet of paper, a packet of cotton wool, a plain white saucer, and a packet of seeds. Elmo looked at the seed packet.

"Alfalfa seeds," he said in a surprised voice.

"Which joke do they come from?" asked Liz, wrinkling her forehead. She picked up the sheet of paper and unfolded it.

"What is it, Liz?" demanded Tom.

"It's the Phantom's shopping list," Liz said. "Book titles on one side, equipment needed for the jokes on the other. See? 'How to Paint Cats — toy cat, paints, brush. The Wonderful World of Frogs — chocolate frogs.' And so on."

"Very efficient," said Sunny.

"Whose writing is it?" asked Nick eagerly.

"I don't know," murmured Liz. "It's not Mr. Raven's, anyway. Do you recognize the writing, Elmo?"

Elmo shook his head. "I don't think I've ever seen any of the library staff's writing. Or not often enough to remember it, anyway."

He looked closely at the list and frowned. "This isn't complete, you know," he said. "The last few jokes are missing. The second-to-last one here is *Teddy Bears' Adventure*. And look at the last one: '*Gardening for Beginners* — cotton wool, saucer, alfalfa sprouts.' That must be a joke that the Phantom planned but hasn't done yet."

"He was going to grow some alfalfa sprouts on wet cotton wool for the next joke," said Tom. "But he never did it. He played the Noah's ark trick on Richelle instead. *Bible Stories for Children* isn't on this list, though."

"*Hamlet* and *Bleak House* aren't here, either," said Elmo. "Why not?"

They looked at each other, confused. But I already knew the answer. I looked up at them from where I was sitting on the floor. "Only the nice jokes are on the list," I pointed out. "The ones that didn't hurt people."

"Why would that be?" Sunny asked. "It doesn't make sense."

"Yes, it does," Liz said slowly. "What if the Phantom started the jokes for fun — and then something happened to make him angry, really angry? Wouldn't he stop planning? Maybe he'd just start lashing out on impulse, wanting to cause real damage."

There was silence for a moment. I think everyone had started to feel very uncomfortable. I certainly had.

Then, suddenly, there was a click from the door. Someone was coming in! Tom yelped a warning. Sunny sprang to the door. Like lightning, Elmo swept papers over the stuff on the floor, to hide it.

"It's only me," called Miss Spicer, as the door swung open. She stared around at us anxiously. Her hair was already escaping from its pins and straggling wildly around her face. I concentrated on looking normal.

"Something wrong, Miss Spicer?" asked Liz, in a casual voice that sounded very fake to me.

"There's something wrong with the computer terminals," Miss Spicer quavered.

I felt a stab of panic. If the computers were freezing up, I might not be able to find *The A–Z of Desserts*. Disaster!

"I was hoping one of you could help," Miss Spicer was going on, her little black eyes darting around to look at us all and finally fixing hopefully on Nick. "I know that some of you are good with computers, but I'm not, and the library opens in a few minutes."

"I'll have a look at them," said Nick.

"I'll come with you," I said. I couldn't just wait there, without knowing what was happening.

We left the storeroom and walked past the empty borrowing desk. "Where are Mr. Kelly and Mr. Raven?" I asked, looking around.

"Oh, they left, dear, about a quarter of an hour ago. Mr. Raven was only dropping in to remind me about the record book. And to check on that awful painting. And Mr. Kelly doesn't usually work on Saturday morning. He just wanted to make sure things were okay." Her voice was sharp.

"Oh," I said. She was obviously angry because both men had checked up on her. But it didn't really surprise me that they had. I wasn't sure how Miss Spicer would cope by herself if something went wrong.

Nick and I walked softly to the computer terminals. Sure

enough, the screens were gray and dead. It was so quiet that I could almost *hear* the silence. It was so creepy. But Nick didn't seem to notice.

"First rule of fixing a computer, Richelle," he said importantly, "is to check all the connections before you start messing around."

He started fiddling with the wires at the back of the computers. "These are secure," he said. "I'll check the surge protector."

He followed the wires to the floor, and with a triumphant "Aha!" flicked a switch. With a loud beep, all three computers began to hum in a comforting way.

"But that's so simple!" I said, in amazement and relief.

Nick shrugged. "People forget to check these things," he explained. He sighed in satisfaction.

"Oh, you've done it!" said Miss Spicer, scuttling over.

"Easy," he said. "The surge protectors were turned off."

Her forehead wrinkled. "That's impossible," she said. "We never turn the surge protectors off. Just the individual computers. I'm sure. I didn't . . ." Her voice trailed away. I exchanged looks with Nick.

"Never mind, we all forget things," he said politely. "Now all we need to do is start up the program."

"Could you do that for me, dear?" she said gratefully.

Nick slid into the chair attached to the computer desk and reached for the mouse. It wasn't there.

"The mouse cord goes into the desk drawer," I pointed out.

"Funny that they call it a mouse, isn't it?" chattered Miss Spicer. "I suppose it does look like a little mouse, with a cord for a tail."

She wandered away again, out to the front doors to open the library to the public. I looked after her. Weird, I thought to myself.

Nick opened the drawer a bit and started pulling at the mouse cord. "The mouse is stuck right at the back," he said. "How did it get in there?"

I heard Miss Spicer opening the big front doors, and behind me, like an echo, I heard the noise of the desk drawer sliding wide open. And then there was silence.

"Richelle?" Nick said in a small voice.

"Mmm? What?" I answered, looking at my nails.

"M . . . mouse. Mouse!"

"I know what a mouse is, thanks," I answered, bored with all this computer business. My nails definitely needed filing. I could do it tonight, when I got home, or . . .

"*Mouse!*" yelled Nick. He grabbed my shoulders and spun me around, pointing wildly. His eyes looked crazy. I struggled to get out of his grip.

"Nick, what's your problem? What's wrong with . . ." The words died on my lips as I saw what he was pointing at.

It took me a second to realize. And then I screamed, and Nick screamed, and we both sprang backward, eyes fixed on the horrible sight on the desk.

At the end of the cord was a real mouse — a nasty, furry, stiff little mouse. Very, very dead.

14

Bleak mouse

The others came running when they heard us scream. The few people who had just come in from outside stopped uncertainly. Miss Spicer stood frozen, staring. And Frankie appeared beside her.

"Moysten, if this is your idea of a joke, I'll make you regret it for the rest of your life!" yelled Nick. He was furious, but I could see that his hands were shaking. I was just speechless.

"I know nothing about this! I swear!" said Tom in amazement.

"Well, just get rid of it then!" said Nick through clenched teeth.

"Have you got a plastic bag or something, Miss Spicer?" asked Sunny calmly. "We'll wrap it up and put it in the trash."

"What do you mean, 'we'?" I said in a small voice. I wasn't going anywhere near that mouse.

The librarian looked around in a dazed sort of way.

"I'm here, Mary," said Frankie gently. He took her arm and guided her toward the front desk. "I'll bring something," he called back to Sunny over his shoulder. "Don't touch it."

The people who had just come in began backing out again. They'd obviously decided that the library was not a good place to be.

"Did the Phantom kill the mousie?" we heard a little kid ask, in a piercing voice. His parents shushed him and walked faster. Soon the reading room was empty again. Except for us.

"If the Phantom did this, then where's the book that goes with the joke?" muttered Tom. "If you can call it a joke," he added, with a sideways look at Nick and me.

Elmo pulled the drawer all the way open. "It's the *Bleak House* cover again," he said.

He was right. But the "H" in "House" had been roughly changed to "M" with a thick black pen. Now the title read: *Bleak Mouse*.

"That's really sick," said Nick angrily.

Frankie came back with newspaper. He looked very worried and upset.

"Well, my little friend," he said to the mouse, trying to smile as he freed it from the cord and wrapped it up, "I don't know how you managed to escape the trash, but it won't happen twice."

"Is this the mouse that was in the trap yesterday?" asked Elmo.

Frankie nodded. "I'd recognize that chewed ear anywhere," he said. He wandered off, with the horrible little package in his hand.

"Poor mouse," sighed Liz.

"Poor us, you mean!" I muttered. Now that the shock was over, I felt full of energy, and I was thinking quickly. I looked around. "Come back to the storeroom," I whispered. "We've got to talk."

○

"Listen, we've been all wrong," I said when we were safely huddled together in the storeroom, with a heavy box jammed against the closed door. "We were saying earlier that the Phantom must be one of the temp staff, but he can't be!"

"What do you mean?" asked Liz, bewildered.

I looked at Tom, Elmo, and Nick. "We were here yesterday, when Mr. Raven found the storeroom all messed up, and Frankie fished out the mouse in the trap. Right?"

They nodded, frowning.

"Mr. Raven said that the library had become a bleak house. And Tom said . . ."

"I said, 'The mouse has become rather bleak as well. It's a bleak mouse,' and then I called you and Nick murophobes," said Tom loudly. "Okay, okay, so I was stupid. I was just trying to —"

"No, no," I interrupted impatiently. "I'm not picking on you, Tom. I'm saying —"

"You're saying that the Phantom must have heard what Tom said," Nick broke in, his eyes gleaming with angry excitement. "It gave him the idea for the mouse trick today. And the temp staff weren't there. The only suspects who were there were . . ."

"Miss Spicer, Frankie, Mr. Kelly, and Raven Mad," I finished for him.

Liz gasped.

"They'd all know you're good with computers, Nick," I went

on. "And all of them heard what you said this morning about the Phantom being a loser, and about how you were going to catch him. . . ."

"All of them heard the police say Help-for-Hire Inc. was good at solving mysteries, too," Elmo put in.

"So the Phantom set a trap," I said. My spine prickled as I said the words. "Put the dead mouse on the end of the computer mouse cord. Got the *Bleak House* cover and changed 'House' to 'Mouse.' Turned off the computers, knowing that Nick, who hated mice, would go and fix them. . . ."

"So the joke was planted deliberately to scare me off!" hissed Nick. His face was pale with anger.

"And to scare the rest of us off with you, I'd say," said Elmo grimly. "It must be obvious to all of them that we work as a team."

"This is awful," whispered Liz. "We shouldn't have taken this job."

"We could go," suggested Tom hopefully.

"No!" exclaimed Nick. "This is personal. How dare anyone try and scare us off?"

"That's right," I said, surprised to hear the words coming out of my own mouth. "We're going to finish this job and collect our money and leave. But before we leave we're going to call Greta Vortek and tell her about that plastic bag full of evidence so she can come and see it for herself. That'll show the Phantom!"

I looked around and was pleased to see everyone nodding — even Tom, who was looking at me quite admiringly. I started working at top speed, picking up pages and throwing them into boxes as fast as I could. Everyone else began to do the same.

"You know, I think the Phantom's going crazy," said practical Sunny, as she worked. "The way the jokes have changed from nice to nasty – it's like someone who's losing their grip on reality."

"The jokes haven't just changed from nice to nasty, either," said Elmo. "They've changed from being clever and well-thought-out to being weak and really unfunny. Like the man covered in flour who was supposed to be the ghost from *Hamlet*."

"Yeah. At first, the Phantom took a book and created a joke with it," said Tom. "He made a joke to go with the book. Like *Alice in Wonderland* and the tea-party, or *Buying and Selling for Profit* with the money inside it."

We all nodded.

"But it's like the last few jokes have been done the other way around," he went on. "As if the Phantom's thought, what's something bad I can do? And then found a book that vaguely went part way with the trick he'd thought of."

"Like I told you," Sunny said. "He's losing his grip."

I gritted my teeth. I had my own ideas about who the Phantom was. But I didn't want to talk about it. I didn't even want to *think* about it.

"If the Phantom's crazy, we know who he is, don't we?" said Tom. He said the last two words in Mr. Raven's toneless voice and tucked an imaginary piece of hair behind his ear.

"It's not Mr. Raven," snapped Liz. "We know his handwriting."

"Mr. Kelly's neat enough to be crazy," said Tom, who

suspected anyone who didn't like messes. "He could have come back from vacation in secret."

"From so faraway? I don't think so," said Elmo dryly.

"But that only leaves Frankie and Miss Spicer," Liz wailed.

Still, I didn't say anything.

"Listen, let's try to think what happened on Tuesday," urged Elmo. "That was the day the bucket fell on Richelle's head. That was the day the jokes changed. That day, something turned the Phantom against the library. What was it?"

I couldn't stand it anymore. I had to say what I thought — however shocking it was.

"Mr. Kelly yelled at Miss Spicer on Tuesday when she tried not to accept Mr. Raven's painting," I said slowly. "He said the supervisor was unhappy about the way she was running the library. That she was in danger of being fired. She was really, really angry. And very upset."

They stared at me for a moment.

"It couldn't be Miss Spicer!" Liz exclaimed at last.

"It could be," muttered Tom. "Miss Spicer has always been very protective of the jokes. Like you would be if you'd done them."

"They did attract visitors — at first," said Nick thoughtfully.

"That was probably her plan," Sunny put in. "But then it all went wrong. The jokes made the supervisor even more certain that she was inefficient."

"And on Tuesday, she discovered that she was about to be fired," muttered Elmo. "It tipped her over the edge."

"It's not surprising that the supervisor prefers Kelly," Nick said. "He's younger and much better organized."

Elmo shook his head. "The supervisor *couldn't* think Mr. Kelly would be better than Miss Spicer!" he exclaimed. "She's the perfect librarian for Raven Hill."

"She probably thinks so, too," said Tom. "But it seems the supervisor *does* prefer Mr. Kelly. So Miss Spicer decided to show them how bad it can get."

"I can't believe it," cried Liz. "I can't believe she could be so stupid. Or so . . . unkind."

Unkind. The word seemed to echo in the small, dim room. Then it hung over us, black and menacing.

"She's going crazy," I said. "Haven't you noticed how she just snaps from gentle to angry? It's not normal."

Liz and Elmo looked miserable. They didn't want to face facts.

There was a bang on the storeroom door. Everyone jumped.

"Hey! Open up!" yelled a voice. Miss Spicer's voice.

"Don't let her in," suggested Tom wildly. "She might be armed!"

"Tom, you really are ridiculous sometimes," scoffed Liz. She ran and pulled the box away.

The door creaked open to reveal Miss Spicer, staring in at us. She gave a high-pitched laugh. Her hair was flying in all directions. Liz took a step backward.

She is crazy, I thought wildly. *What if she really does have a gun?* I held my breath.

But then I saw that the librarian was holding a tray of drinks. "I thought you'd like some refreshments, dear," she said, handing the tray to Liz.

She looked around the room. "You're off to a great start in here!" she said with a kind smile. "I'm so pleased!"

I looked at her. The smile seemed quite real. She really did seem pleased. I felt confused. Maybe I'd been all wrong about her.

She turned to leave. "I'd suggest you leave the door open in the future," she said. "It seems to be sticking."

"Oh, it's okay," murmured Liz.

Miss Spicer looked back at us over her shoulder. She wasn't smiling anymore. "Now you just do as I say," she said. "You wouldn't want to be trapped in here. Would you?"

Was I the only one who heard the threat in those words? I glanced around at the wary, serious faces around me and knew that I wasn't.

15

Bad feelings

It was one o'clock, so we decided to have lunch. No one felt like going outside where we'd have to talk to Miss Spicer, so we just stayed where we were. We drank the drinks on the tray and ate our sandwiches.

It was a rather silent meal at first because the door was open and we all knew that we could be overheard. But gradually people did start talking, thanks to Tom, who wanted to tell everyone about the newest phobias he'd discovered. His latest favorite was vitriophobia, which he said meant "fear of stepfathers." Tom doesn't get along very well with his stepfather.

"Then there's alektorophobia — fear of chickens, arachibutyrophobia — fear of peanut butter sticking to the roof of your mouth. . . ."

Elmo wrinkled his nose. He had peanut butter sandwiches for lunch.

". . . vermiphobia — fear of worms, and emetophobia — fear of vomiting," Tom went on happily, gulping down the last of one enormous roll and reaching for another.

"Oh, shut up, Moysten!" groaned Nick.

"Nick's got Tomophobia," giggled Sunny.

"Me, too," said Liz, who was looking quite sick.

Soon they were all talking and arguing just as usual. Now was my chance to look up my book. I put down my sandwich, got up, and quietly left the room.

Miss Spicer and Frankie were sitting at the borrowing desk, working on a jigsaw puzzle together. They barely looked at me as I walked quickly past them and hurried to one of the computer terminals.

I checked the desk carefully before I sat down. I felt quite nervous. I would have liked to have had one of the others with me. But however scared I was I couldn't bear the idea of them finding out about my stupid topic. I started typing quickly, and soon *The A–Z of Desserts* and its reference number came up on the screen. But so did two other words: *On loan.*

I stared at the screen in disbelief. After all that effort, the book wasn't in the library at all. It had been borrowed by someone else!

I trailed miserably back to the storeroom. The others were still eating lunch, but I'd completely lost my appetite. Now, on top of everything else, there was no way I could finish my assignment. My last hope was gone.

❋

Nick went to the bathroom and called Officer Vortek from there. She wasn't in, and neither was her partner, but they were expected back in a few hours. Nick said he'd call back. "No point in talking to anyone else," he told us, when he came back. "They're all so busy — and this is Greta's case."

We worked quite steadily for a long time after that. I think everyone was as eager as I was just to finish the job and get away. Slowly but surely the shoe boxes filled up, and more and more carpet came into view.

"We're almost done," sighed Sunny with relief.

"I've got an idea," said Nick.

"Uh-oh," said Tom.

"No, it's a good idea," Nick insisted. "After this, let's all go and get a pizza and a video, and go on to my house."

"Yeah!" we all shouted. We went back to work feeling much happier. And, quite soon after that, the carpet was completely clear, except for twenty boxes neatly stacked with pages, all in order.

Nick went back to the bathroom and called Greta Vortek again. But she still wasn't there.

"What'll we do?" whispered Liz, when he got back and told us. "We can't leave the bag here. The Phantom might move it."

"We'll take it with us," Nick breathed. "Drop it off at the police station on our way home. We shouldn't really move it, but leaving it's too risky."

We put the plastic bag carefully at the bottom of Tom's backpack, and left the storeroom. Elmo came out last, carrying one of the shoe boxes.

"I want to borrow this book about the alphabet," he explained. "Ripped or not."

Miss Spicer agreed to let him borrow it, even though it was

in pieces. "It's the least I could do, Elmo dear," she said. "You and your friends have done a marvelous job. Thank you so much."

We all murmured uncomfortably, very aware of the evidence we were smuggling out in Tom's bag. I knew we had to do it, but I couldn't get rid of the feeling that we were being really sneaky. The others obviously felt the same way, because when Miss Spicer handed over our money, even Nick tried to tell her we didn't want it.

"Nonsense!" she insisted. "You must take it. Please!" She pushed the envelope into Elmo's hand and pointed at the jigsaw puzzle. "Look at what Frankie and I have been doing while you've been working," she said. "It seems dreadful, but the booking desk had to be manned, and the library's been so quiet, you see."

We politely looked at the jigsaw puzzle. It was a huge circus scene, very complicated.

"These pieces are tiny," exclaimed Liz.

"I have eyes like a hawk," boasted Frankie.

"He certainly does," nodded Miss Spicer. "I don't know how you do it, Frankie — older than me, and you still don't need glasses."

Frankie beamed and patted her hand.

As we left the library I looked back. The two heads were bent over the jigsaw puzzle again. They made an odd sort of couple, but they certainly seemed very fond of each other.

✿

We stopped by the police station. It was very busy, with people rushing around everywhere. We waited for about fifteen minutes, and then Greta came in and we gave her the Phantom's bag of tricks. We told her where we'd found it and why we'd decided to bring it to her, instead of leaving it where it was.

She said she understood. She promised to check the list against samples of the library staff's handwriting first thing in the morning.

"I feel bad," sighed Liz, as we left. "I sort of wish we'd never found the bag."

"There's nothing we can do about it now," Sunny said sensibly.

"Except cheer up! And stop talking about it," suggested Tom. He stamped really hard in the middle of a puddle and cold rainwater splashed up all over me.

"Oh!" I screamed. "Tom, you idiot, why did you do that?" I ran after him, but he just laughed and ducked behind Liz.

"At least I got you moving!" he called. He jumped in another puddle and wet Liz. And then Nick. So we held him under a tree and shook the wet branches so that water dripped on his head.

By the time we got to Nick's we were quite wet, but happier. Nick's mom gave us towels to dry our clothes, and one to wrap my hair in. We had our pizza and watched our video. We stretched out in front of the fire.

I should have felt quite relaxed. But I didn't. And I could see that no one else did, either.

"Why aren't we happy?" I burst out at last.

"Maybe we all have gelophobia," said Tom miserably. "Fear of laughing," he added, without even waiting for anyone to ask.

"I'm happy," said Sunny, looking anything but. "Happy to be away from the library, anyway."

"Yeah," Nick agreed. "The atmosphere's terrible in that place. You get the feeling that something's building up and about to explode any minute."

Elmo spoke up. "I wish Greta had time to settle this Phantom thing tonight," he said restlessly. "I don't like the idea of it all waiting till the morning. I just feel like something really bad's going to happen. Is that stupid?"

"No, I know what you mean," said Liz.

"I have exactly the same feeling," said Sunny. "And that doesn't often happen to me."

Liz sat up. "Maybe we should go and have a look," she said. "Just to make sure everything's okay."

"It's nine-thirty!" I exclaimed. "It's cold out there. And dark. And thundery."

"Astraphobia," muttered Tom. "Fear of thunderstorms." Everyone ignored him.

"What if something happens in the library?" worried Liz.

"Well, it won't," I said stubbornly. "No one would be crazy enough to go to the library tonight. It's a perfect night for staying home."

"Yeah. And that means that this would be a perfect night for the Phantom to strike," said Nick. "No one around to see."

I fixed my eyes on the fire. Just when we were all warm and comfortable, they wanted to go out again. Well, they could go without me: I wasn't going along with it this time. I wasn't moving from this spot, and nothing my friends could say would make me change my mind.

✿

Fifteen minutes later I was following my so-called friends down the sidewalk. We were one street away from the library, and it was really, really cold. Thunder rumbled overhead. There were flashes of lightning. The air was thick with a fine drizzle that I knew was frizzing my hair into a mass of crazy knots. I felt like a complete sucker.

"Why am I *doing* this?" I asked through chattering teeth.

"Because you know we're right," said Liz.

"Something's got to give, Richelle," added Nick. "The bucket of water, the flour, the ripped-up books, the mouse – the Phantom's 'jokes' are getting more and more vicious, and they're happening more often than they used to."

"Well, this is going to be a big waste of time," I grumbled as we turned the corner.

I was so wrong. Because just at that moment Liz gasped, and Sunny yelled "Quickly!" and then we were all running.

Orange and red light flickered weirdly through the drizzle. The lightning flashed in the glowing sky. And the flames at the library windows burned steadily on.

16

The Phantom unmasked

It was like a nightmare. The lightning lit up the sky, the fire lit up the ground. Flames leaped against the upstairs windows. The attic was burning.

"The rare books!" Elmo yelled.

Nick was talking fast into his phone. "Fire!" I heard him say.

"Fire!" yelled another voice close to my ear. I spun around. It was Mr. Raven, his pale eyes wide and staring.

"My painting!" he groaned.

Then Liz screamed and pointed. "There's someone in there!" she shrieked.

The next minute, Sunny was running to the library doors, pushing them open, and rushing inside. And Mr. Raven was following her.

"What are they *doing*?" I screamed to Liz. "Are they crazy?"

"Raven Hill Library," yelled Nick into the phone at the same time. "It's only the upstairs at the moment, but there's someone inside. Hurry!"

Liz ran to the library doors. "Sunny!" she screamed. "Sunny!"

I tried to pull her back. She struggled with me.

"If Sunny was here, she'd say, 'Don't panic,'" I yelled. "She'd say, 'If you go in there, too, you'll just make things worse.' Wouldn't she? Wouldn't she?"

Liz finally seemed to hear me and nodded. I pulled at her arm. "Sunny's better at this sort of thing than we are. She'll be all right," I said, though I could hear the fear and worry in my own voice.

"I don't know what to do," Liz moaned.

At that moment, we heard sirens in the distance. Then everything happened at once. Two fire engines came speeding down the road, and Sunny and Mr. Raven burst from the library, almost carrying Miss Spicer between them. Miss Spicer was choking and crying, clutching books to her chest. Her hair hung limply around her shoulders.

We all yelled with relief. The fire engines screeched to a stop, and suddenly firefighters were everywhere.

"Upstairs," coughed Miss Spicer, panting for breath. "Upstairs."

A police car pulled up behind the fire engines, and Greta Vortek and Officer Klein got out.

"I found this in there," cried Miss Spicer. With shaking hands she gave a book to Greta. "It's *Rebecca*. There's a fire at the end."

"What were you doing at the library at this time of night, Miss Spicer?" Greta asked.

"I . . . got a phone call," she stammered. "Telling me that something was wrong. But whoever it was hung up right away."

Officer Klein turned to Mr. Raven. "And you, sir?"

Mr. Raven pushed his damp hair behind his ears with bony fingers. "I was just passing by," he said briefly.

Greta looked at us and raised her eyebrows.

"We . . . we just came to see everything was all right," said Liz. "We were afraid that the Phantom would . . ." Her voice trailed off.

"What's that you're carrying?" Officer Klein asked Sunny.

"Miss Spicer was holding it when we found her," she murmured, handing him a large metal can.

"Kerosene," he said to Greta.

"I found it," babbled Miss Spicer. "With the book . . ."

Frankie came running up, puffing and panting. "Mary! Are you okay?" he called, putting his arm around her. "Why weren't you home? I was worried sick."

"Where were you? I tried to call you. I left a message on your answering machine," wailed Miss Spicer.

A car pulled up across the road. Mr. Kelly got out. He was wearing a dark suit and tie. His orange hair was soaking wet and plastered across his bald patch.

"Good grief, what's happening?" he roared, looking from us to the fire and back again.

"What are *you* doing here, Mr. Kelly?" asked Officer Klein, pushing back his cap. Things were getting a bit too complicated for his liking.

"I thought I'd just check the library on my way home," said Mr. Kelly. He looked up at the burning library again and covered his face with his hands. "Oh, Mary," he mumbled. "How could you do it?"

Miss Spicer just moaned.

I expected Frankie to leap to Miss Spicer's defense. But to my surprise, he didn't. And to my even greater surprise, I saw that his arm had tightened around her, and tears were running down his cheeks.

I felt as though I was in a dream. There was something odd about this scene. Something wrong. I just couldn't think what it was.

Greta glanced at us, and then back at Miss Spicer. "We have a list of Phantom jokes, found in a bag with items used for those jokes, Miss Spicer," she said gently. "The list is in your handwriting, isn't it?" She paused. We all knew she was bluffing. But it worked.

"Yes," quavered Miss Spicer. "Yes." And she bowed her head. "I was the Phantom," she whispered. "It was me."

I felt shocked. All along I'd been right. Little Miss Spicer was the Phantom. *You really can't judge a book by its cover,* I thought to myself. I realized that Mr. Kelly was speaking, slowly and reluctantly.

"I saw you set up the teddy bear joke, Mary," he said. His bristly mustache jumped up and down, and his eyes were sad. "I didn't want to get you into trouble with the supervisor. Or with the police. I tried to help you, to warn you to stop. But you didn't stop. Why, Mary? Why?"

Miss Spicer sobbed against Frankie's shoulder. "It's not what you think, Pierce," she wept. "I started the jokes. I wanted to make the library a happy place. Encourage the children especially to come and enjoy reading. But the teddy bear joke was the last one I did. Someone else did all the others, I swear. I was afraid to own up in case you thought I'd done them all."

I could see that the police didn't believe her. After all, she'd lied from the start. And there was so much evidence to prove that she was lying now. There was an empty bag of flour in the plastic bag of Phantom tricks. She'd been found in the burning library, holding the kerosene can.

Greta led her away to a police car.

A firefighter came out of the library and told Officer Klein that the fire was under control. Nearly out, in fact. He congratulated us for having saved the library — and probably the life of Miss Spicer — by raising the alarm so quickly. Luckily, the fire had only been burning for a very short time when the alarm was raised. It had apparently started when someone threw kerosene on a painting on the wall, and then a match, the firefighter said.

"My painting," breathed Mr. Raven. He shook his head helplessly. "She hated it," he murmured. "She didn't want it in the library. But did she have to destroy it?"

Officer Klein looked grave. "Can you confirm that Miss Spicer disliked the painting in the attic?" he asked us, Frankie, and Mr. Kelly.

I nodded with all the others, feeling like a sneak.

He asked us to come to the police station right away to make statements, then went back to join Greta.

It was terrible. We stood and watched as the police car drove away. Miss Spicer looked back at us through the window. She looked very small, very lonely, and very scared.

✿

Frankie drove Liz, Elmo, Sunny, and me to the police station in Miss Spicer's car, while Mr. Raven, Tom, and Nick went with Mr. Kelly.

I felt miserable, and Elmo and Liz felt even worse.

"It's not our fault," said Sunny. "Miss Spicer had to be stopped. Someone could have been killed."

"You're right," muttered Frankie unhappily, his eyes fixed to the road. "I should have found a way to stop it myself. I knew Mary was the Phantom all along."

"She told you?" I gasped.

He shook his head. "I found the bag of Phantom stuff in the storeroom," he said. "I'm in and out of there all the time. I found the bag, and the list, and I know what Mary's writing looks like." He smiled sadly. "But I didn't tell her I knew. And I never even thought about telling the cops. Even when the jokes got . . . not so nice."

He shook his head. "This is all my fault," he groaned. "All my fault."

"You'll have to tell the police what you know," said Sunny quietly.

Frankie bit his lip. "Yeah," he mumbled. He thought for a moment. "Listen," he said. "Could you do something for me? I don't trust cops. I don't want Mary getting in more trouble because they've written down what I've said wrongly. Can one of you kids read over my statement when they've typed it? I've lost my glasses at home, you see, and —"

I gasped. He glanced at me quickly, then looked back at the road.

"Frankie, you have eyes like a hawk," I said quietly. "You said so, this afternoon, when you were doing the jigsaw puzzle. You don't need glasses."

"I do! I mean, I . . ." stammered Frankie. He fell silent.

"And you didn't know what my magazine article was about," I went on. "It was a quiz, but you thought it had something to do with the alphabet." Suddenly that strange conversation on Wednesday afternoon was making sense to me.

"You thought it was about the alphabet because you saw A, B, and C on the quiz choices, didn't you?" I took a deep breath. "You can't read, can you, Frankie?" I asked.

"Richelle!" exclaimed Liz. But Frankie was nodding, and tears were springing into his eyes.

"What's the point in pretending anymore?" he said, wiping the tears away. "You're right. I've tried to hide it for a long, long time. But it gets harder and harder — always pretending that I've lost my glasses or hurt my hand, just so people won't ask me to read or write things."

There was silence in the car. I think all of us were trying to take it in.

"How did it happen, Frankie?" asked Elmo at last. "Didn't you go to school?"

"I grew up in the circus. We were always traveling, and I never paid much attention to schoolwork. It didn't seem important at the time."

Frankie's hands clenched on the wheel. His usually jolly face was sad and angry. "But now it's hard to get a job," he muttered. "It's hard to do anything. Everything depends on reading and writing. And people are cruel. It's bad enough being so short, without people thinking I'm stupid as well. I didn't want anyone to find out."

I could understand that. He must have felt so embarrassed.

"It's nothing to be ashamed of, really, though," Liz burst out. "Lots of people have the same problem."

Frankie nodded. "That's what Mary said when she found out a couple of months ago. She's been wonderful. She said she'd help me. She told me stories from famous books. And last week she helped me enroll in a special reading and writing class for adults. So I could learn to read the books for myself."

"That's great!" exclaimed Elmo. But Frankie shook his head.

"Mary felt sorry for me," he muttered. "And that's why all this is my fault. I'm sure she started the Phantom jokes because she was trying to encourage kids to come to the library. To make reading fun for them, so they wouldn't end up like me. And then when she got upset, when Kelly started picking on her — things just went too far."

"Don't blame yourself," cried Liz.

"Miss Spicer made her own decision to change the jokes from kind to unkind," said Sunny quietly.

Elmo murmured in agreement.

Only a few minutes before, I would have agreed, too. But suddenly I wasn't so sure. Why?

It was because of something Frankie had just said. It had to be.

But what was it?

17

Never judge a book by its cover

By the time we parked outside the police station, I was still thinking.

"You're very quiet, Richelle," Liz whispered to me as we went inside. "Are you feeling that sad about Miss Spicer? I didn't think you liked her very much. And you said she was the Phantom."

"I know," I whispered back. "But . . . for some reason I'm not feeling so certain about her now. I've started thinking that maybe she's telling the truth after all. Maybe she only did some of the jokes. The nice ones."

She stared at me, and I could see hope in her eyes. "Do you really think so?" she asked.

"Well, remember how Sunny said that the Phantom's personality had changed completely?" I said. "And how Elmo said that the bad jokes weren't nearly as clever or well-thought out as the good ones? If there were *two* Phantoms, it all makes sense."

We went in through the police station door. Mr. Raven, Mr. Kelly, and Miss Spicer were already there, with Nick and Tom and Officer Klein. Frankie hurried in behind us and went up to

Miss Spicer. He put his arm around her. Again I noticed what a cute little couple they made.

Then I suddenly remembered what it was that Frankie had said to make me think Miss Spicer might be innocent after all. He'd said, "It's bad enough being so short, without people thinking I'm stupid as well."

How could I not have seen it before!

I gripped Liz's arm. "It's true!" I hissed in her ear. "Miss Spicer *didn't* do the Noah's ark joke. She didn't do the Hamlet joke with the flour. And I'll bet she didn't tear up the books, or plant the dead mouse, or set fire to the library, either!"

Liz's eyes were wide. "The flour packet was in the plastic bag with everything else!" she said.

"It was put there!" I insisted. "Don't you see, Liz? Someone else did all the bad tricks, and they fixed it so Miss Spicer would get the blame!"

"Who fixed it?" whispered Liz. "Who?"

My eyes darted around the room. Mr. Kelly was talking to Mr. Raven and Frankie. His mustache twitched as he spoke, and his ginger hair, resting heavily on his forehead, moved up and down every time he raised his eyebrows. He stroked it from time to time as if it comforted him. To me he'd always looked peculiar. But I put that out of my mind. I was determined never to judge a book by its cover again.

My gaze moved to Frankie. To me he'd seemed so jolly — a happy clown, without a worry in the world. But that had been another example of me judging a book by its cover. All the time he'd been hiding a secret that made him sad and angry, and his life very hard.

And Mr. Raven — weird, creepy-looking. A good poet, but a bad painter, Miss Spicer had said. Very imaginative, Liz had said. Interesting, Elmo had said. What was inside Mr. Raven's cover?

Greta came into the room. "Miss Spicer?" she said. "Could you come with me, please?"

"Richelle?" hissed Liz.

I clenched my fists in frustration. What *was* it that had seemed so odd tonight at the fire? I knew the answer was there.

Images began to flash through my mind. People and things I'd seen in the last week at the library. Tiny details like pieces of a jigsaw puzzle that I hadn't even known I was putting together. I saw the scene at the fire replayed again and again in my head, faster and faster.

I looked around the room again. In frustration, I ran my hand through my frizzy, knotty hair. . . .

And then, suddenly, everything fell into place.

I jumped to my feet.

"Greta, you have to let Miss Spicer go," I said loudly. "She's telling the truth. The last Phantom joke she did was the teddy bears' adventure."

Greta sighed. "Richelle —" she began.

"I can prove it," I insisted. "Just listen to me. Please!" I looked around quickly. My friends were looking worried. I didn't blame them.

"We don't have time for this," muttered Officer Klein.

Greta folded her arms. "Richelle," she said sternly. "We'll give you two minutes. But it had better be good."

I took a deep breath. "Miss Spicer couldn't possibly have put the bucket of water or the bag of flour on top of the bathroom doors. She's much too short."

There was a second of shocked silence.

"She used a ladder," suggested Greta, recovering.

I shook my head. "The library ladder is broken," I explained. "Isn't that right, Frankie?"

"Yes," said Frankie nervously.

"A chair, then," snapped Officer Klein.

I shook my head. "All the chairs in the library are connected to the desks," I said. "They can't be moved. Isn't that right, Mr. Kelly?"

He nodded.

I turned back to Greta. "And besides, Liz was in the ladies' room only ten minutes before the bucket of water fell on me. The trick was set up quickly. There was no time to run around with things to stand on. Miss Spicer couldn't have done it. Frankie couldn't have, either. The only people tall enough were Mr. Kelly and Mr. Raven."

I saw Mr. Kelly's eyebrows shoot up in shock.

"Now just a minute!" said Mr. Raven, in a much louder voice than his usual one. "What exactly are you leading up to, Richelle?"

"My hair," I said. "I'm leading up to my hair."

Officer Klein rolled his eyes. Liz was tugging urgently at my arm. But I'd gone this far. I had to go on.

"I pay a lot of attention to people's looks." I said. "Especially their hair, because I worry a lot about my own. This week I've noticed that Mr. Kelly's hair is very like mine. It goes frizzy when it's raining. But now, my hair is frizzy, and his is lying wet and flat across his bald patch. Why is that?"

Everyone turned to look at Mr. Kelly. He flushed a dull red. I hurried on.

"On Tuesday, Mr. Kelly and I had something else in common. I got a cut forehead, and he got a bruise in the middle of his bald patch when he bumped his head on the low doorway into the attic."

"I fail to see," said Mr. Kelly, "what this has to do with —"

"Just be patient, sir," said Greta calmly. "Go on, Richelle."

I swallowed. "Mr. Kelly didn't bother hiding his bruise, but I spent the week trying to hide the bandage I had over my cut," I said. "The only thing that worked was to get my hair really wet and plaster it across my forehead."

I waved my arm at Mr. Kelly. "You can't see the top of Mr. Kelly's head now, because his hair's been wet and plastered over his bald spot," I hurried on. "The last time I saw his bruise, it had faded to a very light brown. Let's see what color it is now!"

Mr. Kelly just stood there.

"Would you brush your hair aside, please, sir?" Greta asked politely.

With a face like thunder, Mr. Kelly did as she asked. And there, in all its glory, was a big, bright red lump, right in the middle of his head.

"That bump's very recent," said Officer Klein, staring at it.

"That's because he did it just a few hours ago," I said. "He rang Miss Spicer anonymously, to make her come to the library. Then he ran to light the fire so it would be just starting when she arrived. But in his hurry he did what he'd done many times before in that attic — he hit his head on the top of the door."

"Nonsense!" barked Mr. Kelly. "I . . . hit my head getting out of my car."

"Well, why did you hide the bump?" I asked quietly.

There was a second of complete silence. Then, suddenly, Mr. Kelly lunged for the door.

He almost made it. But not quite. Officer Klein had him firmly by the arm in a second. He struggled to get away, shouting.

"It's not fair," he roared, red in the face. "Mary Spicer was making a circus out of the library. She didn't deserve to be running it. She had to be stopped."

"You framed her!" yelled Frankie angrily.

"You tried to *burn* the *library!*" shouted Elmo, Liz, and Miss Spicer together.

"I knew the fire wouldn't have a chance to take hold! There wouldn't be too much damage!" thundered Mr. Kelly. "But I'd had enough. I had to get Mary arrested and fired somehow."

"Pierce!" Miss Spicer squeaked, and burst into tears.

He glared at her. "I deserved to be head librarian!" he snarled. "I kept telling the supervisor that. But those stupid Phantom jokes were attracting more and more people. Making you look too successful! I had to get rid of you. I had to!"

And at that point, he was hauled away, completely and utterly defeated.

It's hard to describe what happened next. The room seemed to erupt with yells, cheers, and congratulations. My head was whirling around. Miss Spicer and Frankie were thanking me a million times. Mr. Raven was shaking my hand. Greta was banging me on the back. The gang were all hugging me. It was probably the most attention I'd ever gotten in my life.

It made it all worthwhile. Almost.

❀

Miss Spicer is still head librarian at Raven Hill Library. And now that she and Frankie are married, he sometimes dresses up in one of his old clown costumes and does tricks for the kids in the library. As he says, not every little kid loves reading right from the start. Sometimes they just need a bit of encouragement. He told me the other day that his own reading classes are going really well, which is great.

As for my assignment — that Saturday night, when all the excitement was over, I finally found the courage to tell everyone my topic. And you'll never guess what happened. They all said, "You should have told us!"

Liz's mom has friends who own a cake shop. Frankie once worked for a baker and knew all about making doughnuts. And even my mother knew what the big mystery is: how they get the hole in the middle. They don't just cut a bit out of the middle, like I'd always thought. The doughnut's cooked in that shape. The batter is actually piped through a ring-shaped mold into hot oil to cook.

I should have known. When I'd asked Mr. Raven what the mystery about doughnuts was, that sneaky man told me that if I thought about it, I'd "work the *whole* thing out." That was the clue. But he meant "hole," not "whole." I should have listened more carefully.

And I guess I should have listened to Tom as well, because his overdue library book turned out to be — you guessed it — *The A–Z of Desserts.* He said he fell in love with the picture of a chocolate eclair on the cover. He finally found the book on Sunday, all caught up in his blankets. Shows how often he makes his bed.

But as it turned out we didn't have to finish the assignment after all. Because on Monday we were told that Mr. Raven had left. He'd decided to give up teaching.

He wrote our class a letter apologizing for leaving so suddenly. He said the fire had made him realize that his destiny lay elsewhere. And he included a hand-painted raven bookmark for me — he said I was the class mystery champion. Liz, who'd done an awful lot of research on elephants, was quite annoyed that I'd managed to top the class without opening a single book.

It was strange to think that for a minute I'd suspected that Mr. Raven had set fire to the library out of revenge because he couldn't work there anymore, and because Miss Spicer hadn't liked his "Unkindness" painting. It was only for a minute, of course, because I knew, really, that never in a million years would he have let that painting burn. He was much too proud of it.

We aren't sure what he ended up doing after he left Raven Hill. There was a rumor that he was working at a library in England, and another that he'd bought an antique bookshop in the country. But no one really knows. To this day, that little mystery remains unsolved.

But you never know. We might find out one day. Liz says life is not an open book. She's says that's why it's exciting. No one knows what they'll find on the next page.

Maybe. But there's one thing I know absolutely for sure. Whatever it is, it's likely to spell more trouble for Help-for-Hire Inc.!

About the Author

EMILY RODDA is the author of the hugely successful Deltora books, including the Deltora Quest series, the Deltora Shadowlands series, the Dragons of Deltora series, *The Deltora Book of Monsters*, and *Tales of Deltora*. She lives in Australia.

HIDE
OUR VALUABLES.
ON'T WALK THE STREETS ALONE.

x troublemakers are on the
ose in Raven Hill. And they
ok a lot like the Help-for-Hire
ng! If the real gang doesn't
gure out who's trying to set
em up, it could mean the end
their friendships—and a
hole lot more!

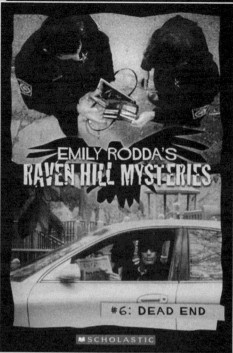

EMILY RODDA'S
RAVEN HILL MYSTERIES

#6: DEAD END

SCHOLASTIC

Welcome to Raven Hill...
where danger means
business.

SCHOLASTIC

www.scholastic.com